CW01454627

Reflection of Evil

The Ink Links

authorHOUSE®

AuthorHouse™
1663 Liberty Drive
Bloomington, IN 47403
www.authorhouse.com
Phone: 1-800-839-8640

Published by AuthorHouse   12/18/2012

ISBN: 978-1-4772-5044-0 (sc)
ISBN: 978-1-4772-5045-7 (hc)
ISBN: 978-1-4772-5046-4 (e)

Contents

Introducing the Ink Links

A small group of students from Huxlow Science College and Irthlingborough Junior School in Northamptonshire accepted a huge challenge—to create their own book for children.

They were named The Ink Links.

Entirely written and illustrated by these talented youngsters *Reflection of Evil* is a fast-paced adventure story for boys and girls between the ages of 8 and 12.

Meet the Hunter twins Amelia and Daniel, their friend Helix plus numerous other characters, some good, some bad and some completely evil.

Authors and Illustrators

The Junior Ink Links	The Senior Ink Links
Hannah Hood	Naomi Busby
Marcus Hood	Holly Farrar
Louise Mastropierro	Michaela O'Callaghan
Olivia Morton	Skye Thornton
Alex Rukaber	Katie Vaughan
Eleanor Sim	Lucy Vaughan
Ellie Waters	Joel Wylie
Editor	Katherine Adams
Illustrations and front cover	Sara McGuire

And some of their characters

Amelia

Daniel

Helix

The Sage

The Riddlemaster

Gibble

Gabble

Vivienne

Prologue

Daniel slammed the creaky attic door behind him and ran up the stairs to his den. He kicked a box of Christmas decorations out of his way and threw himself down on to the old sofa.

"I can't believe she would accuse me of that," he muttered to himself. "Why would I even want her diary?" Daniel sat up, leaning over to pick up his sketchbook from the rickety coffee table beside him. Out of the corner of his eye he saw a glint; clutching his sketch book he rushed over to investigate.

"Oh, it's just a stupid, grotty old mirror," he muttered, drawing the cloth from it.

The mirror had a large jagged crack down the centre with a missing shard. Daniel leaned towards the gap and peered into it.

"I can see something," he thought, getting as close as he could to the mirror. As he leaned forward hesitantly, he caught his sleeve on the crack and the mirror shattered revealing a swirling vortex. To his utter horror his movement was uncontrollable as he was pulled into the mass and despite his fierce resistance he slipped into the void.

Chapter 1: Looking into the Dream

Amelia walked into her room and saw her diary on the shelf. "Oh great! Now I've got to say sorry!" She picked it up and went to search the house. Amelia began looking in Daniel's room yet there was no sign of him; next she went towards the kitchen but before she got there, a shimmer of light caught her eye . . . the attic stairs had pieces of glass on them. Holding the diary closely to her chest with both arms, she started walking up the stairs. Reaching the top she stopped, stunned, and the diary fell from her hands. Amelia saw a swirling abyss; a bottomless pit. The diary was being slowly pulled towards it and so was Amelia. She clung to a wooden beam whilst the diary disappeared but she couldn't hold on any longer. When Amelia opened her eyes, her blurred sight started to clear and she saw something leaning over her. She let out a shriek and the creature immediately mimicked her; it stepped back hastily, tripped over Amelia's diary and fell flat on its face. Amelia laughed. "What are you?" she asked reaching out in disbelief. The little creature also reached towards her; it seemed to be copying her movements.

"M . . . mm . . . me. . . a . . . Amarku," it stuttered. Its large brown eyes glistened in a puppy-dog way, its fur was long and hazel in colour and its ears big and floppy. Amelia wanted to pick it up and cuddle it.

"What's an Amarku?" she asked.

"It's, it's, it's me," it replied with a cute but cheeky grin.

"Do you have a name?"

"Gibble, me Gibble. What's yours?" Gibble asked.

"Amelia Hunter." He perked up.

"All humans called Hunter then?"

"What do you mean?" replied Amelia in confusion.

"B . . . boy called Hunter, he come through shiny rock." He pointed behind her and she looked round.

"Daniel's here!" She muttered under her breath.

Looking around her she noticed that the trees all had dark green trunks and purple leaves, the grass was blue, the sky was a delicate green and there were two silver suns in the sky.

"Wow, this place is cool!" she said in astonishment; she stepped forward realising that Daniel must be in trouble. "Where's the other Hunter? Where's my brother?" Gibble stepped back and held his hands to his face.

"Th . . . th . . . they took him."

He shivered in fear as Amelia came forward.

4

"Who?" He jumped back and covered his face.

"Th . . . the henchmen of D . . . D'Angelo!" He shook and Amelia realised she was scaring him; she calmed down.

"Sorry Gibble, I didn't mean to frighten you, but Gibble, do you know where Daniel is?" she finished.

"Me don't know where he is but me know way to evil woman's house," Gibble replied.

"I need to help him! Please help me!" He thought for a moment.

"Come with me, me take you to the Sage." He walked towards the forest and ushered her over. She followed, intrigued to find out who the Sage was.

Gibble guided Amelia through a deep, dark forest. She kept catching her clothes on the purple brambles.

"Ouch!" she shrieked, panicking, thinking that something had caught hold of her. As the brambles cleared, Amelia noticed a black opening in a cliff in the distance.

"That home, that home!" Gibble exclaimed excitedly. A mysterious figure dressed in black emerged from the darkness of the cave.

"Finally, you have returned Gibble, with our guest, the Hunter girl!"

"How did you know we were coming?" exclaimed Amelia.

"I am the Sage, my dear. I know everything." He gestured for her to come forward, holding out a yellow, wrinkly hand in welcome.

Amelia walked forward hesitantly and carefully placed her hand on his.

"Do you know where my brother is?" she asked.

"He is with your rival, known as Vivienne D'Angelo. She is not what she seems; her aim is to steal all the talent from the Hunter family, past and present. She will strip your brother of his talent and take it for her own. You must defeat her or he will be lost forever."

"But how?" Amelia stammered, "and why us?"

"Your family cursed the D'Angelo family many years ago and Vivienne swore revenge. She drinks the tears of her victims to stay young."

The Sage led Amelia into the cave where a fiery green light was burning. Sitting down on a rock, he leaned over the flickering fire and motioned Amelia forward.

"Look deep into the fire and I shall tell you a legend that has been passed down from Sage to Sage." She stared into the fire as the cave became darker. "Every one hundred years, twins of the Hunter family are forced through the mirror into our world to stop the dreaded D'Angelo." In the fire they could see two children fighting an evil sorceress.

"To save your brother, you need to stop her by fulfilling the prophecy before the two suns of our world align. If not, she will destroy this world and use the Amarkus as slaves to help her take control of your world. Amelia saw her life crumbling away in the fire.

"How am I going to do this? I'm only a child."

The Sage sat back from the fire and stared straight into Amelia's eyes.

"Vivienne is not her real name. She has hidden her own name away and it has been lost. To defeat her you must find and reveal her real name. The letters have been scattered over this realm. We know that one letter is where the water meets the sand but I cannot help you any further." Amelia clutched at her sleeve.

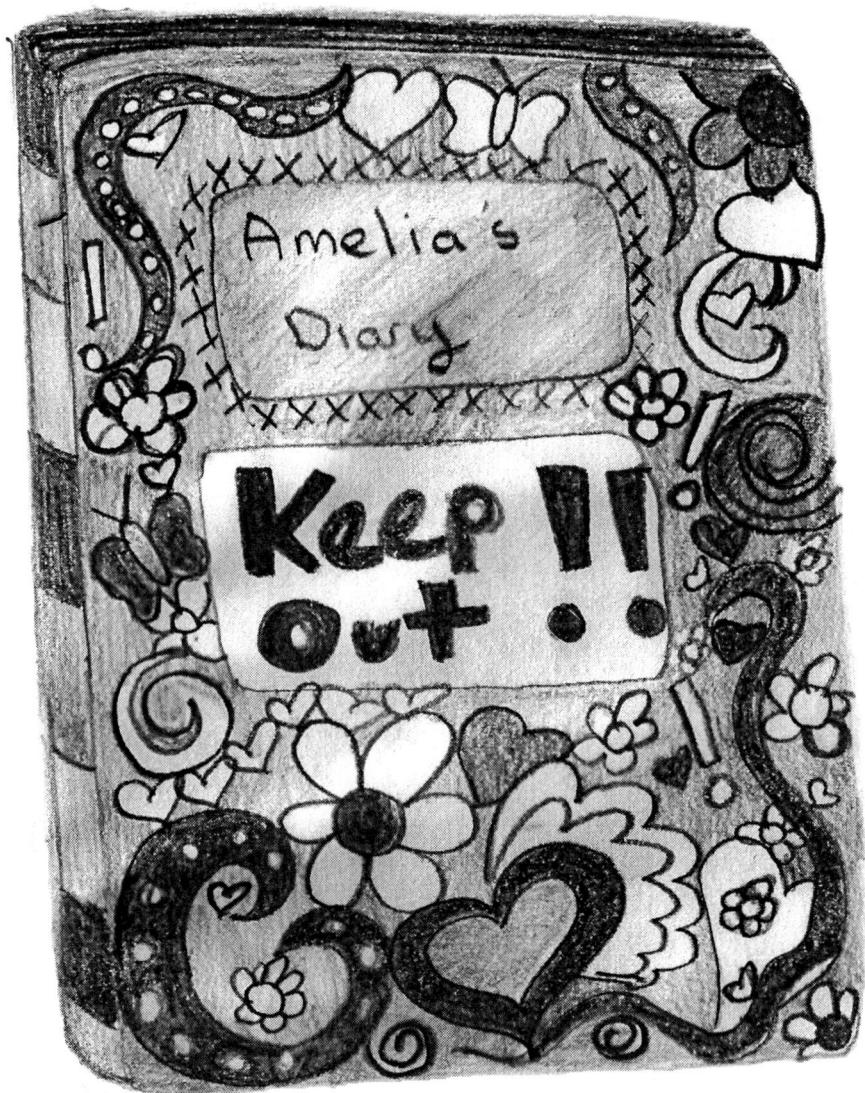

"I can't do this by myself."

"Gibble, m . . . me help." Gibble jumped into her arms. The Sage stood up and showed Amelia a bed in the corner of the cave.

"Sleep! You have got a long day ahead of you." Amelia nodded her head in gratitude as she lay down upon the bed and fell into an exhausted sleep.

Curling up into a ball, Gibble slept peacefully beside Amelia as the Sage began to pack a small brown bag for them. He worked methodically as he had been taught to do, packing a blanket and a small amount of food.

"Gibble will know how to gather more food," he thought as he unravelled an old worn map and placed it at the front of the bag, along with the diary which he had taken from Amelia's slender hands.

Amelia was woken up early by Gibble jumping on her.

"You need to stop jumping on me," she grumbled under her breath.

"You have to leave as soon as possible!" exclaimed the Sage. "You only have sixteen days before the suns align. If you succeed in finding a letter, D'Angelo will make her anger felt. But be cautious of her henchmen, they will cause trouble for you. Good luck, my friends and may fortune guide your steps!"

He stood and watched as they disappeared into the forest. He returned to the cave; the only way he could see them now would be through the fire.

Chapter 2: The Journey Begins

After walking for a while, Gibble and Amelia went over to a shady spot underneath a tree, plonked themselves down, and took a sip of water from the bottle in the brown bag the Sage had given them. Gibble took out the wrinkly map and opened it up, trying not to rip the thin, stained paper: it must have been very old since it was so fragile and torn.

"Y . . . y . . . you can see the mountains and the waterfall and the flowery gardens . . ." Gibble was pointing at all the pleasant places. Amelia had a thought: what about the bad places where Gibble wasn't pointing? She scanned the map like a detective until she saw what looked like a very forbidding place: in the centre of a gigantic river was a small speck of land marked *Lost Island*. Gibble saw where she was pointing and it sent a shiver down his spine.

"No! No! Not that bad place!" he shrieked, "B . . . brings bad thoughts to Gibble's head!"

"We must search everywhere, Gibble, even if it's dangerous," Amelia admitted, trying to be brave. "The Sage said we'd find a letter of Vivienne's name where the water meets the sand." She turned and scooped the protesting creature up into her weak and exhausted arms.

"Put Gibble down!" he screamed, kicking and leaping for his freedom. "M . . . me no want to go horrid island!" as he kicked up a storm of leaves. Amelia grabbed him by the shoulder.

"Look, Gibble, I can't do this on my own! If you want to run, you can, I'm not stopping you. If you do, you could be held responsible for the destruction of two worlds, you understand?" Gibble slowly nodded and Amelia released her grip. "Right, let's move!" She smiled at him. "Thanks for sticking around. Let's head for the river."

Amelia stepped through the forest in the direction of the river, making a big flush of purple leaves hover around her. Gibble dived forward and grasped her hand as tight as an elastic band. Suddenly they heard a crunch that pierced their eardrums like daggers. They realised it was only a dry stick breaking under their feet, but Gibble leaned closer to Amelia. He felt her heart beating as quick as lightning: it sounded like a deathly tune to him! Gibble released his hand from Amelia's and looked around as they walked. The trees' branches were like arms trying to catch them; the leaves were like spies watching them; the tree roots were like kidnappers waiting to trip them up.

Suddenly the bank of the river loomed into view. They stared at the river: it was flowing so slowly it reminded Amelia of thick custard. But it was dark blood red, getting blacker as it neared the shore of the forbidding island in the middle. There were ashes in the water everywhere: thick, black ashes. The two silver suns reflected on the river like glimmering stars.

Amelia and Gibble sat down to rest underneath a towering tree. Suddenly a shadow fell across Amelia's face: she was shocked as a young boy around her own age, sprang out in front of her.

"Who are you and why do you come to my camp?" he called, eyeing Gibble and Amelia suspiciously and drawing his bow and arrow ready for an attack.

"I am Amelia Hunter." She was pleased with how much strength was shown in her voice. "And this is Gibble."

"Oh! Another Hunter the Sage has sent! My name is Helix."

"Helix. What a strange name," thought Amelia.

"How do you know about my quest here?" she asked him, taking her turn to eye the strange camouflaged boy.

"Well," he said, sitting down next to them, "when my mother was young, she was another Hunter. She married my father, Simon Galley, and when they had me, my room was the attic." A picture formed in Gibble and Amelia's mind. "Underneath an old sheet was an ancient, cracked mirror. One morning I was awoken by a strange sensation: the hairs on the back of my neck had risen." Helix spoke whilst looking up at the green sky. "I got out of my bed and followed a noise which led me into the deepest and darkest of all secrets. As I moved towards the mirror, I saw a shard was missing and reached out towards it. Suddenly with no warning, the mirror shattered and a portal opened, dragging all the contents of my room with it."

17

Helix was blinking hard at this point. "Soon after, I arrived in this strange land," he said, pointing at the blue grass and green sky. "I couldn't see anything apart from a fuzzy brownness leaning over me. Then my vision cleared and I saw a small furry creature. He turned out to be an Amarku, just like you," pointing to Gibble, "but he was called Gabble."

"G . . . G . . . Gibble not know Gabble! Who that?" He was barely recognisable as he had buried himself under a pile of purple leaves: he had never known there was another of his species in this strange land. Amelia interrupted.

"How long ago did this happen?"

"Several years," replied Helix. "Gabble took me to the Sage, who sent me on a quest to find the letters of Vivienne's real name. But I got captured by her henchmen!" Helix was walking around in agitation, forwards then backwards, forwards then backwards, looking nervous all the time.

"You got captured!" Amelia was positively shocked. "It's our quest too! Please help us—tell us about Vivienne's island."

"Well, when I was first taken there I couldn't really see anything, but my senses told me that this was a bad place. I was led to what seemed like a door made of glass; my captors pushed me inside." Helix acted it all out. "It was a humungous sand timer, turning over and over. I was trapped inside with all Vivienne's other prisoners. We kept crying—we were homesick and despairing and Vivienne collected our tears to keep her young." Helix shuddered at the memory.

"So, tell us how you escaped—was it easy?" Amelia was almost at breaking point.

"No, it wasn't easy but my furry friend Gabble helped! He came every day (he'd got away before they could catch him) and we made an escape plan. I made a hole where the glass joined the wooden base: it was extremely difficult because I could only do it when that part of the timer was underneath me and I could only work at night. Eventually the sand began to leak out all over the rotten soil surrounding my prison. Whilst the guards were busy repairing the leak, I made my chance count and ran to the river bank. I hid in the trees till nightfall when the guards gave up their search. I dashed to the shore where Gabble had found Vivienne's boat and we set sail over the river, back to safety." Amelia was amazed that such a little boy could have done so much. "So now I live here and you do too."

"G . . . G . . . Gibble want to play tickle!" Gibble cried out, furiously tickling Helix's back.

"Can you show us where the boat is now, Helix?" said Amelia, interrupting their game.

"I'm sure it must still be here; I hid it well enough, I think," Helix said, leading them down towards the rotten riverbank.

"What's this here?" Amelia was perching on an enormous crumbling 'rock'.

"That's it! You're a genius, Amelia!" Helix burst over and started pulling off all the decomposing weeds from the damp wood.

"So, are you going to come with us or are you going to back away?"

"I can't face that . . . place ever again! Please don't make me!" Helix backed away.

"OK. I guess this is goodbye then." Amelia was tearful.

"G . . . G . . . Gibble want Helix to come!" Gibble was clinging on to Helix's leg, gripping tightly.

"No, little chum, I can't come." Helix hauled the furry creature off his leg and sat on the sand, waving, as Amelia jumped aboard the boat, dragging a reluctant Gibble with her.

"Bye, Helix and thank you! Stay safe!"

The boat floated, but Amelia was not sure it would hold out. Gibble kept swinging back and forth and repeating, "No, not that bad place!" every so often and curling up in a ball. Minutes later, which seemed like hours, they safely reached the shore of the island, not knowing what awaited them in this weird and bleak place.

Amelia and Gibble stepped cautiously out of the boat, careful not to touch the highly polluted water which was so dark, lapping on the shore. The sand was glittering like diamonds and other precious jewels, but it also had a dark side: it was littered with tiny bones.

"H . . . h . . . human bones?" questioned Gibble, squealing in horror as Amelia nodded. Then out of the corner of her eye, she spotted a strange shadow moving about in the distance.

Suddenly the air filled with smoke. The shadow that Amelia had noticed tapped her on the back. When she jumped round, nobody was there! Then the smoke lifted and Amelia and Gibble saw him. It was hard to make out what he was like because he was as tall as a pine tree and wore a hat; his shirt was buttoned right up and he wore a red cloak patterned with hypnotic golden swirls. He held a gold staff.

"Don't be afraid! I'm the Riddlemaster," he boomed. "I've been expecting you: I'm friends with the Sage and he sent a message to say you were on your way. I've always wanted to defeat Vivienne since I was little. Now come with me to my home; I have something for you." Amelia and Gibble suspiciously followed, not knowing what would happen next . . .

They looked around the Riddlemaster's home: it was a pretty barren place with greeny-grey walls and no pictures. The Riddlemaster handed Amelia a tea-stained piece of parchment filled with gold ink runes which were changing colour every so often.

"What's this?" asked Amelia as she touched the gold lettering. She heard a small sizzling sound when her fingers touched the runes.

"G . . . G . . . Gibble read! Gibble read!" screamed Gibble, starting to get annoyed because he was being left out. As Amelia touched the lettering, it transformed from ancient runes to modern-day English.

"Only a member of the Hunter family can read it," explained the Riddlemaster. Excitedly Amelia went on:

"I begin with E
And end with E,
Usually only contain one letter,
But I'm not the letter E."

Amelia read with no expression. Gibble had dozed off!

"Stop it! This is serious! 'I begin with E . . . ' What could it mean?" An eerie silence filled the air.

"You must go! Go! Before Vivienne finds you!" the Riddlemaster ushered Amelia and Gibble out of the door.

"I begin with E . . . I usually only contain one letter . . ." Outside, Amelia was speaking with confusion.

"E . . . e . . . envelopes contain letters," Gibble sounded dazed.

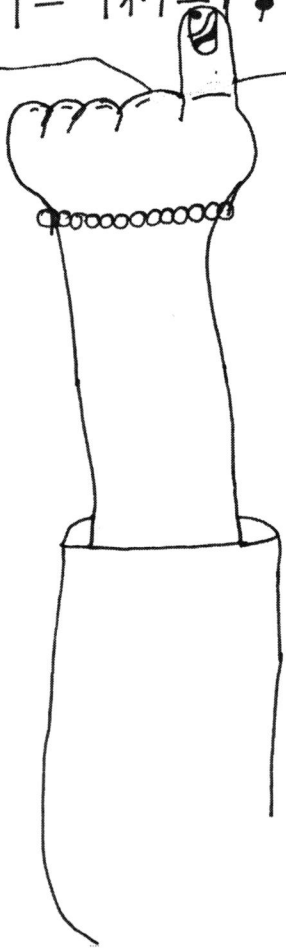

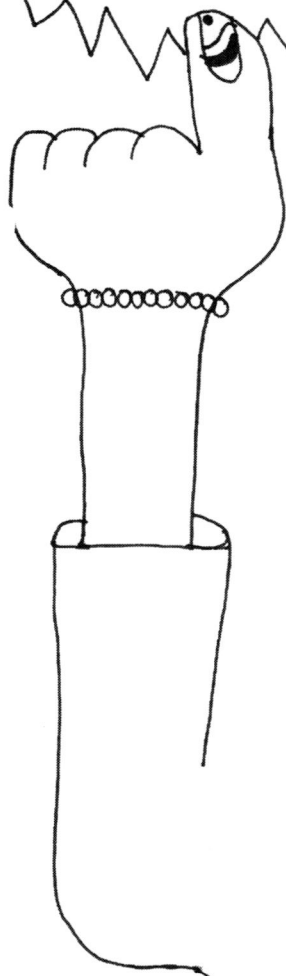

"That's it! Gibble, you're wonderful! *Envelope* begins with E and ends with E and usually contains one letter!" She hugged him with enthusiasm.

"Gibble need to breathe, please!" he cried.

"We'll find an envelope where the water meets the sand," Amelia said, remembering what the Sage had told them.

Rushing down to the river bank, they started a frantic search. Nothing! There was no envelope in sight. Suddenly, Amelia spotted a glint coming from the sand and called out.

"Gibble, will you go and see what that is, please?" Gibble bounded over and started to dig with his dog-like paws until he revealed a dirty, glass bottle. Sealed inside, Amelia could just make out the faint outline of an *envelope*. Taking off the top, she squeezed in her finger and thumb and, painstakingly, retrieved the paper. Carefully, they opened the envelope and stared cautiously at the queer gold runes. Rubbing her finger over the lettering, Amelia watched as two letter Ns appeared. Gibble was jumping up and down in excitement.

"We . . . we found them!" he kept repeating. Amelia opened her diary and carefully wrote the two letters inside.

* * *

Back in his cave, the Sage was staring into the fire. With a wave of relief, he saw Amelia and Gibble find the letters. But Vivienne, at home on the island, was furious. She had sensed that Amelia had written the two letters in her diary. She snapped into a tantrum of uncontrollable rage and as she was storming around, she smashed a pot with mysterious runes inscribed on it. When it hit the floor, an eerie black fog rose from the obliterated remnants. It soon expanded to engulf the whole room. Vivienne grinned as it seeped out of the windows like flour from a sieve. Within minutes, it had engulfed the world in a blanket of darkness. Amelia, standing on the shore, shuddered; she clutched her diary to her chest for comfort. Gibble was nowhere to be seen . . .

Eventually, the darkness cleared and Amelia sprinted to Gibble's side, patting him on the shoulder. She gulped. They had won this round but the next would be a lot harder . . .

Chapter 3: Watched

Amelia and Gibble jumped back into the boat, happy to get off that dreaded island. As the boat began to move, the waves of the river became more violent and the wind whipped viciously, rocking the boat back and forth. Gibble stumbled over his own feet and, with a wail of terror, fell over the side. Amelia grabbed his ankle and Gibble whimpered as she hauled him back to safety.

The wind threw the little boat against rocks and pieces of driftwood. Gibble and Amelia were truly terrified as a giant wave lifted the crumbling wreck of a boat and thrust it on to the shore. Amelia clawed her way up the river bank towards Gibble, her vision fading in and out. She sank to the ground, her mind spinning dizzily and she rolled on to her back. As darkness obscured her vision, she saw a dark figure bending over her.

Peering out from behind a rock, a creature similar to Gibble turned away sorrowfully. His metal ankle strap gave him a shock sending a sharp needle-like pain through his leg.

"Sorry, mistress," he sighed under his breath . . .

* * *

Daniel's eyes burst open, fear racking his whole body; he couldn't quite shake off the feeling that his twin was in trouble. He looked around the glass chamber that was his prison and at the terrifying shadows beyond it. He could not move; he was immobilised by the weight of sand pulling him back every time he tried to move.

The shadows moved forward, blurs formed shapes; shapes forming people . . . It was them . . . the faces flashing in his memory, between unconsciousness. A high-pitched scream coming from a girl beside him brought him back to his senses. Her eyes were blood-shot as she looked straight at him and whispered, "They have come to collect our tears" . . .

* * *

Amelia woke up to find Helix bending over her.

"Aahh! What happened?" Amelia asked sitting up and rubbing her head.

"You got caught up in a river wreck," Helix replied, breathing deeply.

"But, how did we survive?" she asked anxiously. Helix reached out his hand to help Amelia up.

"From what I saw you two were crying and BOOM you're both on shore."

"Boom?" she repeated, giving him a strange look, "Boys!" She pulled Gibble to his feet and said, "What now?"

"G . . . G . . . Gibble stay with Helix," he said firmly. "Y . . . y . . . you too dangerous!"

"Please help us Helix, I need to save my brother," Amelia pleaded.

"At least you have a brother!" Helix answered. "My twin Hannah died when we were born."

"I'm sorry that you lost your sister, but I don't want to lose my twin too." Tears welled up in Amelia's eyes.

"No, no, no. Don't cry," Helix nervously stammered. He waved his hands at her, clumsily patting her shoulder. "Fine", he sighed, "I'll do it!" Gibble squealed as the last of his hope of going home died. He followed them sulkily along the river bank.

"We need some more letters of Vivienne's real name," Amelia cried out in despair.

"Gabble kept talking about letters," Helix said. "Can't remember which one it was though."

"How can you forget?" she glared at him accusingly.

"I don't know. Don't yell at me. I can't think straight. I think it was a D. No, a P. Yes a P."

At that moment Vivienne's henchman pounced out of a bush throwing Helix into a nearby tree. Amelia was terrified and couldn't move; she heard Helix groaning as the henchman stretched out his arms and crept towards her. She attempted to run away but as she stood up, she tripped over Gibble, smashing her elbows against a log of wood. She could hardly feel the pain as she looked straight into the henchman's sharp silver eyes. She couldn't do anything. His pale face was struck with a sly smile.

"Well, well what have we here? You must be Amelia, the other Hunter," he whispered.

"Wait! So you know where Daniel is?" Amelia asked, narrowing her eyes furiously. Disregarding her question, he grabbed her hair, dragging her onto her feet. She struggled, but his hands were firmly gripped around her shoulders. Gibble ran over and sank his teeth into the man's ankle, clinging on like a dog with his bone. The man viciously shook his leg but could not dislodge the determined little Amarku. Suddenly the man's eyes widened, letting Amelia slip through his hands on to the ground; he let out a wail of agony before collapsing, creating a loud thud. Amelia looked up to see Helix standing over the unconscious henchman with a plank of wood in his hands.

"Thanks guys," said Amelia shakily.

Helix used his penknife to slash at some vines. After using them to tie the henchman up, they wrapped the vines around the tree. Helix picked up Gibble and headed in the opposite direction from where the henchman had appeared.

"Slow down," Amelia shouted, running after Helix.

"We have to get out of here. I know a cave which can shelter us. It is quite near here," Helix said, pushing his way past an abnormally large bush.

Thirty minutes later Amelia decided it wasn't 'quite near' but before she could complain, Gibble did it for her.

"Are we there yet?" Helix stopped and sighed.

"You have been on my shoulders the entire time. Anyway, we are here." He pulled aside some foliage to reveal a small opening. The size of the opening was little bigger than Helix, however as they

37

entered, the cave size seemed to expand. At times, small insect-like creatures appeared from cracks in the wall where Gibble liked to wait and flick them off as they came out. It was dry, though quite cold and until Helix had lit a branch and placed it in one of the cracks on the wall, there was very little light. Despite these things, Amelia was not ungrateful, for it was shelter from the weather and the creatures outside.

As Helix looked around, memories from the past flashed before his eyes and the sound of long-silenced screams echoed through his mind. He'd promised himself he wouldn't come back here, but this time he had no choice. Amelia watched Helix gather sticks and light a fire, her patience wearing thin. She couldn't just sit around doing nothing while her brother could be in serious trouble. She had to do something, anything, if only she knew where the next letter was . . .

Suddenly a scream pierced through the cave, echoing against the walls. Amelia sprinted to where the sound was coming from, only to find Gibble cowering in the corner, frozen with fear.

"Eyes . . . eyes in the shadows!" Gibble muttered to himself over and over again. Amelia looked around with alarm; she looked toward the direction that Gibble was staring but nothing looked back. She put Gibble's outburst down to the fact that it had been a long, strange day. Amelia crouched down next to Gibble and was about to tell him that everything was OK when suddenly she heard it—a menacing screech from within the shadows, and with it a pair of eyes glaring at them.

Helix carried on feeding the fire and when he heard Gibble's scream, he thought nothing of it as the little Amarku was easily shaken up. It was only when he heard Amelia's scream that he was truly worried; they must have been seen by the Grozotas. He knew he had to go to them and fast or something terrible would happen but he was afraid . . . deeply afraid. The last time he came face to face with a Grozota it ended horribly; Gabble had surrendered himself to save him. Remembering how selfless Gabble had been to save him, Helix ran deeper into the cave—towards the Grozotas' tomb—towards his cousin and his new little friend.

The darkness surrounded him as he stepped forward. He yelled out in desperation, "Amelia, Gibble, where are you?" For a moment there was silence but he heard scuffling from up ahead, then a loud shriek from Gibble forced him to run as hard as possible. His heart was thundering as visions from the past played in front of him, remembering the Grozotas and how it felt to be in their clutches. Helix imagined the disgusting Grozotas with their grotesque yeti-like bodies and foul breath shoving Amelia and Gibble into an unimaginable horror.

Helix heard the screams getting closer as he reached a dead-end. He fell to his knees . . . he'd failed again. He reached out in frustration and grabbed the nearest rock, throwing it in a temper. Suddenly there was a large crash and the wall in front of him collapsed revealing a small opening. He heard Amelia and Gibble's screams, louder this time, echoing from beyond the opening. He peered inside, seeing the Grozotas' Totem Pole. He'd found it . . . the opening to the Grozotas' tomb!

He saw the end of one of the Grozotas' sharp tails, but when the monsters saw him they snapped a vine and a huge rock crashed to the floor sealing them apart. Helix faintly hit the rock, hopelessly. He heard a pebble kicked behind him and turned around sharply to see . . .

"Gabble! You're OK!" Gabble looked at him solemnly, whilst Helix remembered.

"Why did you send us here?" Gabble sighed with regret.

"Forget about letter P, I wrong. I sorry Helix." Helix stepped back in shock as Gabble took out a bundle of rope.

"Wha . . . what are you talking about?"

"I the slave of Vivienne; the Grozotas took me to her and now I can't escape." Gabble showed the electrified ankle strap, and Helix stood stunned as Gabble prepared to pounce.

While Amelia and Gibble were in grave danger in the Grozotas' tomb and Helix was trapped by his closest friend, the two suns were slowly beginning to align.

Chapter 4: Fire, Fire, Show me the Way!

Amelia gasped as the Grozota tightened its grip around her waist. So this is the end, Amelia thought.

"Hoooowwl!" came a menacing call from a wolf just outside. The Grozota put Amelia down and let out a deafening roar. Amelia frowned. All of the other Grozotas were following suit. Amelia rushed over to Gibble, who had turned white as a ghost, as they watched the Grozotas group together and tumble out into the moonlight, snapping and snarling. The gap in the rock closed.

"What was that all about?" Amelia gasped.

"M . . . me think . . . me think . . ." Gibble shuddered but Amelia could see where he was going.

"They had to go hunting? I think so too." Amelia stared at the desolate surroundings. "But right now we need a way out."

*   *   *

The Sage peered into the fire to find out how Amelia and Gibble were getting on in their quest. He was shocked to see them trapped in the Grozotas' tomb. He could sense trouble. He knew that if he didn't do something soon, the suns would align and they would never be able to get back into their dimension! He could see that Amelia was struggling in the dark, eerie cave, and he could see the goose bumps forming on her arms. Suddenly he knew what to do. He could see a small crack in the jagged rock wall.

"Maybe I could somehow get Amelia to do something to open up the wall and escape," he pondered. Suddenly he noticed a flat piece of rock, hanging like a blank canvas waiting to be painted on. It gave him an idea: he could send a message on it to Amelia and Gibble! He stretched out his index finger and wiggled and waved it around in a mystical way. Suddenly, a bright, golden, continuous spark flew out from his finger tip like a lightning bolt. With the spark he engraved the words *move backwards* onto the smooth stone. He had created a trigger behind her which would open a portal in the crack in the rock wall.

*   *   *

Move Backwards

Amelia was blinded by a bright light which appeared out of nowhere. When she regained her eyesight, she saw runes scribbled on the wall which she was sure had not been there before. As she rubbed her finger over them, the runes changed to letters which spelt out the words *move backwards*. As she did so, she felt a soft breeze on the back of her neck and turning round, she saw the impossible: a way out! She cautiously peered through the gap and could see silvery beams of moonlight from two moons in the dark sky. She could smell fresh air.

She and Gibble were extremely relieved to be out in the open and Gibble started rolling in the fresh, blue grass like a puppy. The moonlight from the two moons was so bright that they could see owls sitting eagerly in their bulky trees, their enormous eyes scanning the ground in search of prey, and packs of wolves fleeing desperately from the ravenous groups of Grozotas. One owl was perched up on the highest branch of a gnarled, old oak tree: it seemed like a wise, old creature and they wondered if somehow he could help them. Suddenly the owl spoke.

"Ah, we meet at last," he said with a certain worried tone in his voice. Amelia was stunned—an owl who could talk!

"You have come to find the . . ." his voice broke off as a deafening crack echoed in the dark sky. Within a second, a luminous fire came out of nowhere slashing the trunk of the tree and separating the branches from the rest. As Amelia and Gibble ducked behind a rock in fright, they could see the owl flying far away.

"Great! Now we'll never find out what he was going to say," Amelia thought to herself.

They were looking at the large oak, with just its trunk standing in its roots. Smoke had filled the misty night air as the branches had fallen into a big log pile.

"G . . . Gibble confused," he whispered to Amelia.

"Me too," she answered. At that point, the owl flew back and perched on Amelia's shoulder.

"This tree is special." He paused and looked around as if to check if anyone was watching, then continued, "When Vivienne was young, she planted this tree and it holds a secret within it."

"But why would she want to chop it in half?" Amelia interrupted.

"Ah, my dear girl, *she* did not send the fire, but instead your friend the Sage did."

"But why would he try and kill us?"

"He didn't try and kill you—instead he did you a favour. Just look at the rings in the trunk and you will see." And with those final words he flew away.

"Well, we know what to do then," Amelia said as she strode towards the trunk, brushing charred, hot wood shavings off the top with her hand. Symbols soon became clear, like some kind of ancient language.

"M . . . me confused," said Gibble, "too, too tired," he yawned sleepily.

"Let's copy it into my diary and ask the Riddlemaster what it means in the morning. It's time to get some sleep now." Several minutes after looking for a place to sleep, Amelia found a hollow tree with a yellow, cushiony base.

"Here, this'll do." They settled down for the night.

* * *

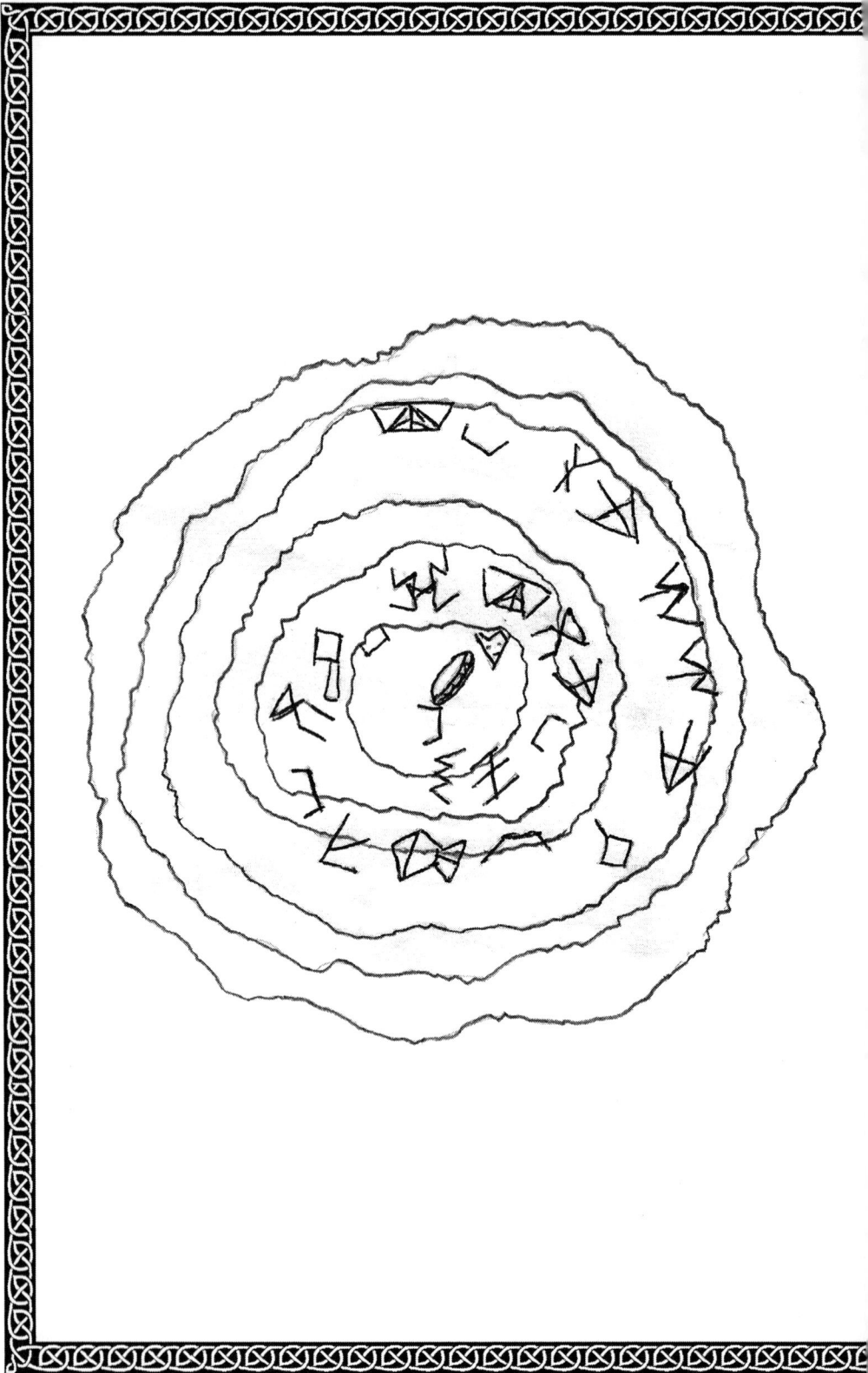

In the morning, Amelia picked out of the back-pack two apples.

"W . . . what that?" Gibble asked.

"An apple for brekkie!" Both of them laughed.

The owl suddenly flew swiftly over to them and settled comfortably on a rough branch. Amelia moved closer to him, asking him to take a message to the Riddlemaster. She ripped the page containing the symbols from her diary, wrote a message to the Riddlemaster and handed it to the owl who grasped it in his beak and flew away, forcing the wind to let him through.

The owl saw the Riddlemaster's house and flying onto the window-sill, he pecked impatiently on the window to attract the attention of the Master who was sitting in a gloomy corner at a messy desk. He snatched the paper out of the owl's beak, and realising that this was no ordinary writing, he walked over to his dusty bookcase. After doing a tuneful knock on the wooden side, a bookworm wriggled out between two books: he was an acidic green and wore humungous glasses and a bright red tie, which covered most of his slimy body.

"Would you help me find the right book for us to solve this mystery, please?" asked the Riddlemaster, showing the bookworm the page from Amelia's diary. In no time at all, the Master was placing a book called *Translations of the Ages* on his dangerously unsanded, wooden desk.

"Hmm," he thought, "C.B.A. translations; Amarku translations; aha! Ancient Runes translations!" He tapped his fingers on the page translating the runes to modern English and quickly scribbling it down, he handed it to the owl. "Mr. Owl, your post!" The owl pecked at the paper then flew away to find Amelia and Gibble.

"My name contains the letter D," read Amelia. "Yes! We have another letter!" she cried, as she wrote it down in her diary.

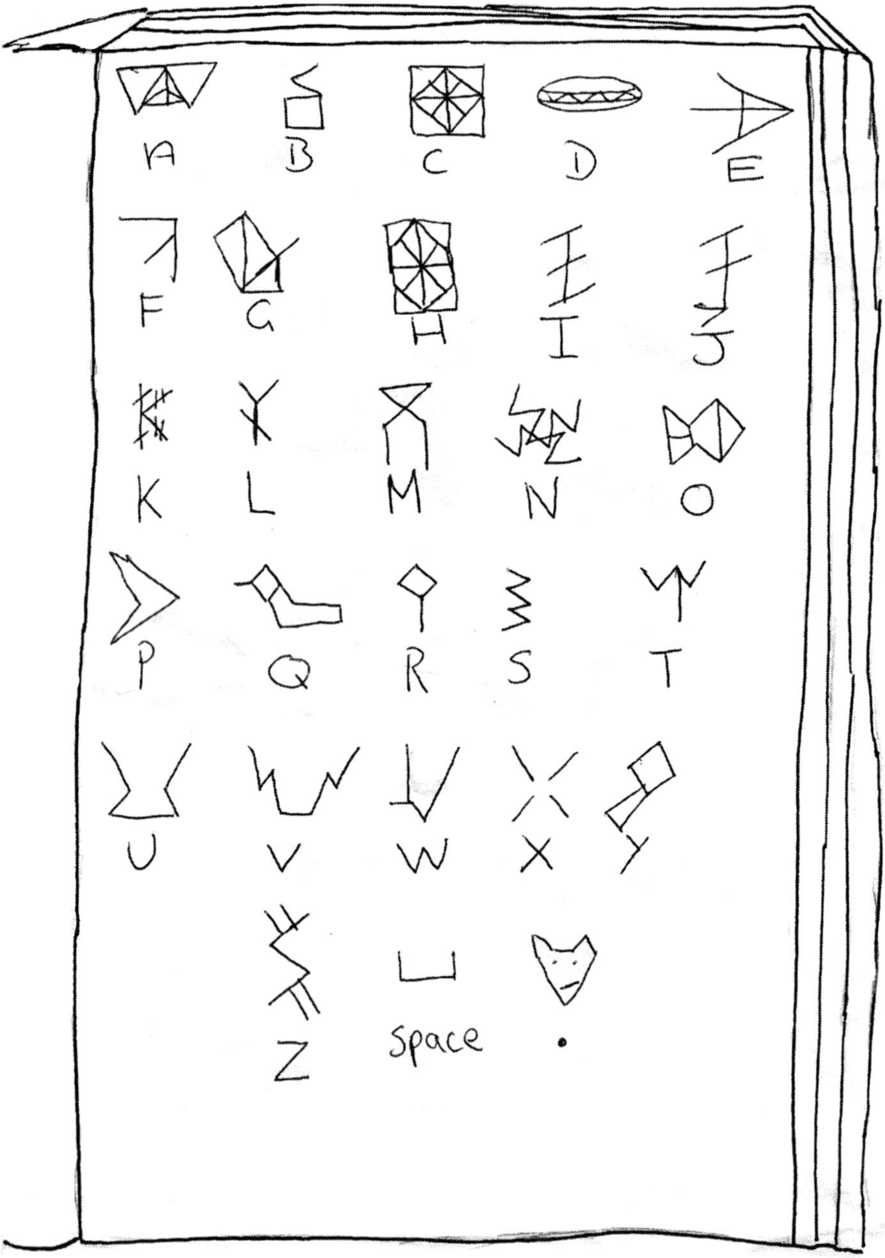

A B C D E

F G H I J

K L M N O

P Q R S T

U V W X

Y Z space

*   *   *

"Blasted Grozotas ruining everything!" Vivienne screamed furiously into her mirror. She used her mirror to see what was happening in her world and she had seen Amelia writing the 'D' in her diary. Vivienne threw the mirror into the ground. As the shards went flying everywhere, a murky grey smoke seeped out from the debris. Vivienne grinned smugly as it flew out of the window and into the sunset.

The smoke fell in pillars onto the unsuspecting Grozotas and as it disappeared, the monstrous beasts shrank. They grew smaller and smaller until they were no bigger than pin-heads. Amelia was watching from a safe distance and she gasped in shock as the miniscule creatures retreated fearfully into their tomb. A thought hit Amelia: if Vivienne could do this, why didn't she just destroy the two of them?

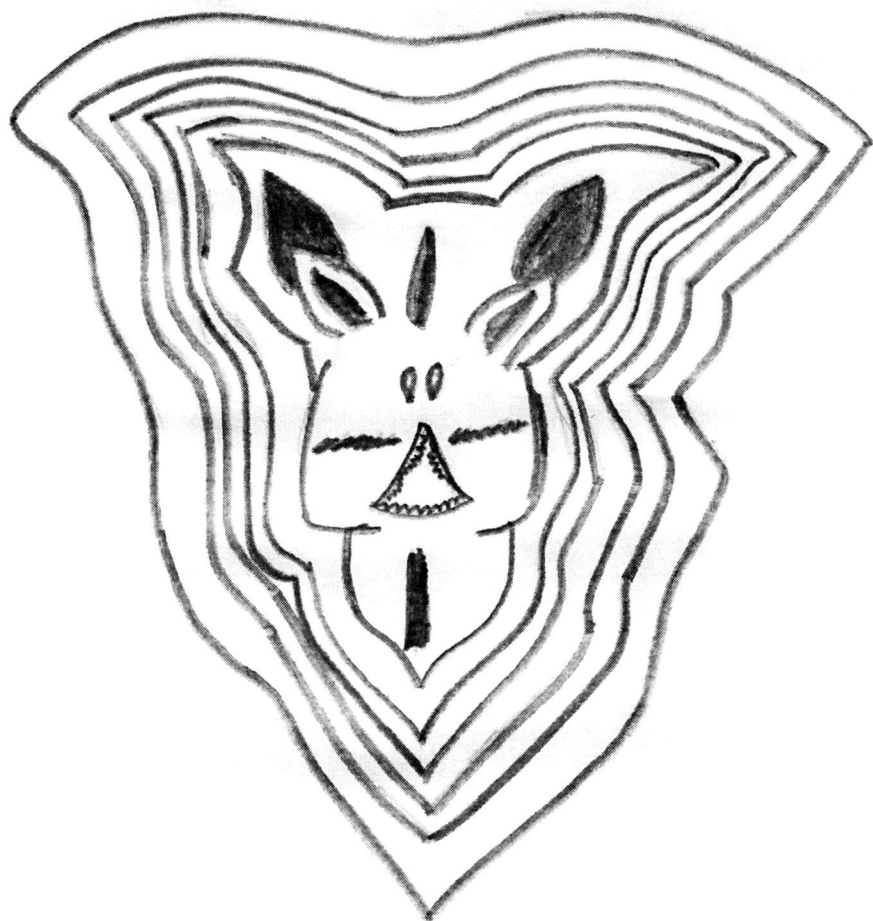

Even in the most beautiful ponds
Can lay the most disgusting scum

Chapter 5: The Beast Within

Outside the cave, Helix and Gabble had been grappling. They heard the wolves howl as they approached them; Helix and Gabble stopped mid-movement and looked around in confusion, backing cautiously away from each other.

Suddenly they heard a thudding sound and scuffling from the cave, realising the Grozotas were coming. Helix and Gabble whipped around looking towards the cave entrance. Gabble rushed and climbed a nearby tree. Helix hesitated only a second before a growl from the cave spurred him into action and he followed.

The wolves retreated, turning and running as they realised they were to become prey themselves. Grozotas shoved out of the cave, snapping and snarling aggressively. They stopped suddenly and sniffed the air. Helix and Gabble held their breath as Grozotas approached the tree they were in, moving closer and closer. A howling wolf broke the tension and the Grozotas leapt into action, rushing after them.

As the wolves fled with the Grozotas snapping and snarling close behind them, Helix slithered quickly down the tree and took to his heels, leaving Gabble stranded. Helix made his way around the tomb and was shocked to find the huge crack. After a second he sighed with relief.

"They must have escaped!" Turning around he realised he couldn't see more than a few feet in front of him; it had become so dark, he decided to rest for now and look for them in the morning.

He was awakened by a large fluffy warmth sitting on his chest. "H . . . he wake, he wake!" Gibble chimed.

"So you always sleep on the floor," chuckled Amelia to Helix, "I've never yet seen you sleep on a bed. No wonder you look so ugly, you never get any beauty sleep."

"Well, when you're on the run from a demon witch, a bed's quite hard to carry around. See how pretty you look then." Amelia scowled.

"Fine, you win." She held out her hand to pull him up. "Now to find my brother." Helix groaned as he took her hand and got up.

"Let's get going then." He stretched before starting off. "This way." Amelia smiled and followed him, pulling the reluctant Amarku along.

They trudged through the forest as Helix led the way.

"So Amelia, what's your plan?" Helix looked up at the blazing suns edging together.

"Well . . . Save Daniel!" He could tell she didn't have a clue just by looking at her.

"Right, and the letters?" A small noise came out of her mouth signalling she didn't know that either.

"Fantastic! This should be easy then!" She frowned at his obvious sarcasm and looked down at the trembling Amarku. Scooping him up into her arms, she exclaimed, "Don't worry Gibble, I'll protect you and we will defeat Vivienne!" He buried his head into her shoulder "OK . . . OK . . ." She stroked him and smiled warmly at the small soft creature.

Amelia looked forwards to the path ahead, the end out of sight, vanishing into the dark, dense forest. Her skin crawled at the sight of the tall tree limbs and shadows that danced within them.

"Are you sure this is the only way to Vivienne's castle?" Amelia asked Helix, voice quivering.

"Unless you would rather cross the chasm of lost souls, this is the only way," Helix replied bluntly. Amelia's eyes widened with fear. She really didn't want to enter the depths of the forest ahead. It was the only way to save Daniel, so she had no choice. Amelia placed Gibble on the ground next to her, took his hand and began on the long winding path.

Helix detested this forest with a passion: too many bad memories; there were few places in this twisted world without bad memories. Helix walked slightly behind Amelia and Gibble; he envied her innocence, unmarred by life. Every tree creak seemed to mimic moans of past ghosts; it would be worth it in the end when they had found all the letters to Vivienne's true name and her reign over the mirror world would end.

Every rustle from within the trees made Amelia jump; she didn't like the feeling of being trapped, of not being able to see ten paces in front of her. Daylight seemed miles away when every direction in sight was shrouded by the shadows of the ancient trees. Amelia looked down at the muttering Amarku beside her.

"W . . . watching. The trees, th . . . they watch. Always th . . . they watch." Amelia looked up at the trees, seeing them in a new sinister light. The dark trees were scaly and had thousands of beady eyes. Amelia had felt something watching her, but she never suspected the trees themselves. Just as things were starting to look hopeless, Amelia spotted an opening in the trees. She burst into a sprint, desperate to feel the light bathe her skin and longing for the terrible itching that the trees gave her to vanish.

That's when she saw it . . .

They approached the old rickety gates, which led to Vivienne's castle; they were covered in thick ivy and looked creepy. As they pushed the gates open, their eyes glanced across the deep aubergine coloured lake that was to the right of them and flowed up to the castle; the lake also continued up to the centre of the winding path. As they looked across the lake, there was no sign of life around for miles. They proceeded along the winding path that was made of broken pieces of stone from decades earlier and there were some stones missing that had been worn out over the years. Above them were the draping, dark leaves of the willow trees over their heads as they walked through. In between the trees were small dark purple bushes in the vague shape of menacing faces, together with gargoyles on plinths. These were there to try and put off any unwanted visitors that entered her castle.

*   *   *

Daniel had given up all hope.

"No-one will rescue me," he thought to himself. "Amelia is probably dead, killed by Vivienne's evil henchmen." He felt there was a hole in his heart which just grew bigger as time went on. As Daniel's hopes grew weaker, his memories of Amelia grew stronger. Like the time she had played with him on the beach instead of going to her friend's, or the time when he lost some money and she gave him some of hers. He thought about the many adventures they'd been on together, when they'd been lost in the forest or captured by the mad scientist . . .

*   *   *

Amelia was scared for Daniel.

"He . . . we had great times together, I wonder if he is OK? Then again he is trapped in an evil villain's castle so of course he's not OK," she thought to herself. Amelia felt there was a huge hole in her

68

heart of how she severely missed Daniel, and how horrible she had been, thinking that he had stolen her diary and it was on her shelf the entire time.

"I wish I had telepathy then I would know how he is," she thought. "Finding him would be the best thing ever."

* * *

Walking closer to the castle, they realised the trees almost looked as if they were rotting one by one as the suns seemingly died leaving nearly no light. Vivienne screeched and threw a vase at the wall. Gibble stopped as he looked up to the demonic castle and shook.

"M . . . me . . . not going in there!" He stepped back as Amelia and Helix turned around and sighed.

"Please, Gibble, we don't have time for this!" Amelia pleaded opening out her arms, but he backed away more before turning around and scrambling towards an opening in the row of hedges beside the path. Helix sprinted after him and Amelia had to follow suit before sighing one last time, thinking "I had been so close to Daniel . . ." Amelia looked around the edge of the maze to see Helix's foot disappearing.

* * *

Vivienne laughed maniacally as she watched her prey scurry into the maze.

"Oh, this is too good!" She turned around to a group of henchmen and ordered, "Release the Kralj!" They hurried off and moments later an ear-piercing roar came from below. Gibble, Amelia and Helix froze.

"What was that?" Helix cried as Gibble screamed in terror and grabbed Amelia's legs. Two red glows appeared from inside the hedges, getting bigger as the charging footsteps got louder.

"THAT'S THE KRALJ. RUN!" They turned and fled further into the maze. As the maze became more complicated, Gibble started to panic.

"Where now? AMELIA! . . . M . . . m . . . me scared." Amelia stopped and turned to see the little Amarku curled up on the floor.

"Gibble!" Amelia sighed, "You have come on an adventure only the bravest would. You've braved the Grozotas' cave and faced the darkness of this castle. You can do it. Gibble?" Once again Gibble found safety in Amelia's strong words. He rose up with the help of Helix and they pressed on until they reached a large space with a crossroads.

"Where to now?" moaned Amelia.

Helix paused for a second and began, "Well I think I can see a . . ." Suddenly they were knocked back against the surrounding hedges by a gigantic heap of monstrous flesh covered in needle-like scales as big as a pencil and as sharp as a dagger. His blood-red eyes could break the heart of any weak man; however Helix stood strong as he gazed in horror at the Kralj!

A roar bellowed out from the Kralj, this time nearly deafening them all. Shortly after it had faded, Helix shouted, "Run!" Amelia nodded in reply as she could not bring herself to speak, dazed from the roar of the Kralj. Suddenly the Kralj tripped on a large tree root which made him slide across the ground. He appeared to drop a key from the chain around his neck. Helix picked it up, thinking it may be of some importance so he threw the key to Amelia, who caught it and took Gibble's hand.

"Be careful Helix!" She hesitated for a second as Helix struggled with the Kralj before Helix shouted, "Just go!" At that moment she yanked a petrified Gibble away from the towering horror.

* * *

As Gibble left with Amelia through one of the exits in the hedge, Helix was left face to face with the Kralj. Silence filled the maze as they locked eyes, then the silence broke and Helix let out a war cry. They both charged at each other before the Kralj swept his claw through the air. Helix slid underneath him, slashing his legs with his dagger, barely leaving a mark. Widening his eyes, Helix looked to the right as the tail of the Kralj swung towards him, knocking him back against the hedge once more.

Lying there as he saw the Kralj turning, unharmed, he thought, "This is it! I have failed Amelia and now I will die a failure." Just then he noticed a large tree nearby, broken but still standing. It had a crack through it and with enough force could still be pulled down.

The Kralj charged as a grin appeared on Helix's battered face. With every ounce of strength left in him, Helix rose up wielding his blade and hacked at the tree. It came crashing down just as the Kralj was nearly upon him, and the tree dealt a crushing blow to the Kralj, falling upon its head. The Kralj crashed to the ground, rumbling the area in a small quake.

The great beast of Vivienne's castle was defeated.

*   *   *

Desperately worried about Helix, Amelia and Gibble ran as far as they could until the roars were nothing but quiet whimpers in the distance. Amelia clutched the key to her chest, struggling for air—running wasn't her finest trait. She realised that they were in a dead end, pushed the key into her pocket and let go of Gibble's shaking hand, causing him to cling to her leg, tripping her up.

"Ow! Gibble!" She rubbed her back as the Amarku didn't talk; he just buried his head into her stomach. "Gibble, its OK, we're alone now." He shook his head and pointed to the hedges where . . . "Oh my . . ." Thousands of . . . millions of red eyes were shining in the area. Quietly she moved to the middle of the path, picking Gibble up along the way. She walked slowly out of the dead end with Gibble in her arms and the eyes followed them. They walked around the maze, terrified by what surrounded them, keeping to the middle of the path as they tried to find a way out.

Amelia looked closely for an exit but couldn't help but get distracted by those eyes; they chilled her to the core. It was then that she saw it.

"Look at that side!" she exclaimed and edged towards it. "There aren't any eyes!" She hesitated but Gibble perked up and jumped on to the hedge, not realising he'd fall through.

"Gibble!" Amelia jumped in after him, although she got a few scratches on her arms she couldn't leave him alone. "Where are . . . ?" She stopped and looked at the immense golden hourglass gleaming in the light.

Amelia's jaw dropped as the silky sand slowly moved and the tapestry tape circled around it. Something moved! She cautiously went closer to see inside. At first she saw nothing but knowing this world, it was probably just a cloak for something, something . . .

"Look! Look!" Gibble pounced at the hourglass and clung to it, interrupting Amelia's thought path. "Someone in there!" She looked intensely trying to find any sign of life. There he was!

"Daniel!" Her face lit up with excitement as she banged on the glass. He lifted his pale face up and whimpered quietly before lowering it slightly so his hair draped across his face. At least he was awake, unlike the other children in the hourglass.

"Amelia! I didn't think you'd come . . ." She was shocked to see her brother so . . . fragile.

"Daniel, it's OK. I will get you out of this. I promise." She smiled reassuringly and started looking about the glass before she heard a gasp from Daniel.

"Key . . ." He slumped down unconscious and Amelia started to panic.

"Quick, Gibble, find the key and I'll find the slot!" Gibble started to search as Amelia frantically hunted for the lock. "There!" She cried and slid down onto her knees. She noticed it curved up at the top and the teeth had to be sharp. "Wait a second!" She dug her hand into her pocket and pulled out the key Helix had thrown to her. It fitted perfectly.

Unlocking the door, she flung it open and heaved Daniel out.

"Daniel, Daniel! Wake up!" She shook him violently and almost cried when his eyes started to flutter open. Amelia almost choked her finally found brother; slightly surprisingly, he chuckled.

"You saved me with an eye." His voice was weak and raspy but Amelia didn't care; she laughed at his smile.

"Which eye?" He pointed to the key and she pulled it back. "Oh yeah, it does look like an eye." Amelia touched the runes and chuckled.

"There's an I inside an eye." She stopped at Daniel's comment.

"An I . . ." she grinned widely. "Another letter!" She pushed her brother gently away and fiddled for her diary, scribbling down the letter.

"Gibble, we've found another letter!" She motioned the Amarku over and saw he was shy at first but gradually came and looked overjoyed.

"W . . . we go home now?" She stroked him and shook her head.

"We still have to defeat Vivienne before the suns align." Amelia stood up and brushed herself off.

"What?" She looked at her brother and opened her mouth to speak but was interrupted by a terrifying scream which caused the only window in the castle to shatter. It was at the top of the central tower, *her* tower, crawling with dark purple vines.

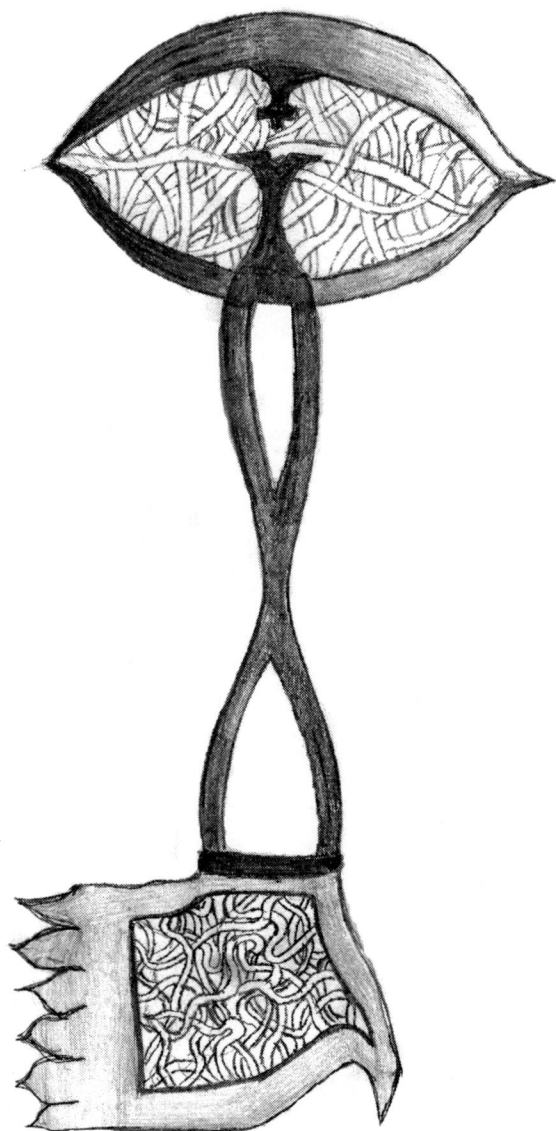

The Ink Links

"I will explain later, Daniel, but we really need to find some more letters. I know there must be more here, but where?"

She attempted to drag Daniel onto his feet while Gibble clung to her legs in desperation.

"Not to be rude, Gibble, but get a grip! I need you!" Nodding his head, he pulled himself off her legs and tried to help Daniel up. Amelia looked at the single black hedge that they had fallen through. She placed her hand against the wall thinking that she might be able to get back through but it rejected her, sending a bolt of lightning through her hand and up her arm. Believing that it was the end for them all, she smashed her hands repeatedly against the side in anger, her tears flowing fast down her face as she screamed.

"How dare you! I hate you! I hate you!" She collapsed on the floor as Gibble tried to calm her down, petting her hair and whispering, "C . . . calm down, Amelia. W . . . we get out of here, me sure of it. He . . . Helix did!"

Daniel, though still frail and tired, was as ready as he ever could be after his experience in the hourglass. He tried to think back to when Vivienne left the hourglass after she had collected his tears but it was all so confusing. He could only remember a small object that was kept around her neck. It shone so brightly that he was stunned by it. It seemed so bright compared to Vivienne and the white box-like room the hourglass was kept in. So lovely, so mesmerising. Suddenly, walking over to Amelia and Gibble he said, "Could that help us—maybe it was a source of power but it couldn't be, could it?"

"What do you mean, Daniel?" Amelia asked.

"I mean, her necklace. Maybe that's it! She always wears it and it seems so magic." Amelia wailed, "Well, it's not going to help us now, is it?" before curling back into a tight ball.

Daniel bent over and gripped her hands, making Amelia stop crying before commanding, "Not to be rude, Amelia but get a grip! I need you!" She stood up, nodding her head and brushing the hair out of her tear-stained face. Daniel wiped it and whispered to her, "Thank you."

They walked around the room, silently trying to find a way out. Gibble was bobbing around, unsure of what to do. He didn't understand what they were doing—they looked so strange, he thought, expecting a door to just appear out of nowhere.

"Think. Think, Daniel," Daniel broke the silence, muttering to himself. "Stop!" He paced up and down, his hands around his head, trying to think. "That's it!" He rushed over to the hourglass and started to pick up the silvery orange sand. Turning back round to Amelia, who was staring at him in confusion, he shouted, "Hurry Up! Get as much sand as you can and put it on the floor a metre from a wall!"

"Why?" Amelia asked, lifting Gibble onto her back.

"Please, just do it!" Daniel said, making a small pile.

Amelia began to help him, unaware of his plan but knowing that it would be wrong to question him. The pile slowly grew as the twins got more and more tired. Finally, Daniel stopped shovelling and put his hand behind Amelia's back pushing her forward to the pile.

"We need to push the sand into the wall at the same time but it rejects it, so you have to push really hard," Daniel said, breathlessly. As they prepared to push, Daniel shouted, "Ready, one, two, three go!" They pushed with all their might, shutting their eyes against the spraying sand that was scorching their faces. Gibble, who was still clinging on to Amelia, covered his face with Amelia's hair. Bright lights burst from the wall, lighting up their determined faces. The sand ran out quickly as they both collapsed onto the floor.

What appeared from the wall then was nothing short of extraordinary.

"Ooh!" Gibble exclaimed with a look of wonder on his face as an intricate glass shape appeared from the wall. Daniel let out a sigh of relief, then took the shape, held Amelia's hand and jabbed the sharp shape into the wall twisting it in as if he was plunging someone in the heart with a dagger. Amelia watched, stunned, as a glass door started to form from the shape; it opened into the broken window frame at the top of Vivienne's Tower. They were out of the room and the maze!

Daniel jumped down onto the floor, covered with shards of glass, leading the way for Amelia who hopped down lightly after him. She had a huge smile on her face while Gibble giggled mischievously on her back. They left the door open in the hope that the other children in the hourglass would escape the same way—there was no time to go back for them now.

Amelia was starting to get worried as she scanned the gardens looking for Helix but he was nowhere to be seen.

"Maybe Vivienne has set something else on him?" she thought. It was then that she realised she could see a huge letter R in the garden path.

"Brilliant," she muttered, scribbling the letter down in her diary.

Amelia turned round worriedly to tell Daniel but he wasn't there. She was scared that Vivienne could have done something to Daniel but before she could fret further, he entered through a rusty iron door to her left. He slipped something small and shiny into his pocket, took Gibble off Amelia's back and smiled at Amelia. She smiled back at him, glowing as she realised she had saved him. He relaxed her but this wasn't the time for relaxing; they had to get out of Vivienne's castle.

They set off as quickly as they could down the winding staircase and into the gardens, searching for Helix as they ran.

"Amelia! There you are!" Helix shouted, running over from the other side of the gardens. He had a deep gash on his forehead and slightly below his bruised red eye was a faint mark of a hand. He hugged her then touched his injuries.

"It was Gabble; Vivienne has made him go mad. He absolutely worships her now and is prepared to kill for her—deadly prepared. It happened a few minutes ago and I have never seen him so menacing and scary—he wasn't even like that in the cave."

"It must have been when we found the letter R!" Amelia said, hugging Helix. Daniel stepped forward.

"Hi! Thanks for looking after my sister." Amelia rolled her eyes.

"Look, introductions later; we really need to leave!" They ran off out of the gate and through the forest, not even stopping when they got tired. They needed to get as far away from the castle and the forest as possible.

After what seemed like hours, they decided to set up camp near a river. The fire was illuminating their faces as Amelia and Helix (with a bit of help from Gibble) explained what their task was and what they had done so far. Amelia had some questions for Daniel as well.

85

How did he know about the glass and how to escape? So before they all fell asleep, she prodded him in the back.

"How . . . ?"

Smiling, he muttered back, "Her henchmen always used to take some of the sand from the hourglass. I remember because when they came to see us, they threw some of it into my eyes. They wanted to make sure I couldn't see what they were doing to get out. All the other children had spent too much time in the hourglass and couldn't see very well anymore."

"But that doesn't explain . . ." Amelia interrupted.

"Let me carry on and I will tell you!" he said, slightly annoyed that she had interrupted him. "Anyway, by the time I had rubbed my eyes and come to my senses, it was all so confusing. I saw this glass door that was definitely not there before. She went through it with her henchmen and closed it behind her then it just disappeared. So it needed sand but what else? Then later I saw you hitting the wall . . ."

"The bolts of lightning!" Amelia whispered in amazement.

"Yes. It was the connection between sand and lightning which made me recall being taught how sand can sometimes turn into glass when lightning hits."

"Wow, so we turned sand into that glass shape which helped us get out!" Amelia said. Helix, who was thought to be asleep, spoke up.

"Why couldn't you just dig your way out like I did?"

"He couldn't. She obviously made it harder to get out after you escaped. She must have been very angry."

"Oh. OK." he huddled back into Gibble who was sleeping soundly. A minute later, Amelia and Daniel could hear Helix's loud snoring.

"R.N.N.D.I. What name could that be Drnni? Indrn?" Daniel said, before falling asleep himself.

*   *   *

As night drew in, Vivienne huffed and fell onto her bed, exhausted. She muttered to herself.

"I wish I could kill those brats right now but I cannot because I am cursed, so I cannot touch those idiot Hunters myself."

Chapter 6: The Good, the Bad and the Amarku

Helix suddenly awoke. Just by glancing at the position of the moons, he knew the time must be almost five o'clock in the morning. Unable to get back to sleep, he decided to go for a wander around the forest, no longer scared of the twisted trees that messed with his soul.

After a while, he saw electric blue, lightning-like sparks in the distance.

"Perhaps I should walk back," he thought, hesitating. But—as soon as he turned around—he felt a rush of fear and heard a creature running . . .

BOOM! Helix was knocked to the ground, his arms bruised and knees grazed and pink. It was Gabble! The sparks came from the anklet he was wearing. A power source?

But before he could even answer himself, Gabble gave him another pound on the back. Helix did everything he could to remove Gabble and destroy the anklet which seemed to have such power over him. Suddenly it struck Helix: Gabble detested the sound that Helix made when he whistled a certain tune! He blew through his lips so hard that the ear-piercing noise could be heard throughout the forest. Gabble staggered back, temporarily deafened. Now was Helix's chance. He dived in towards Gabble's legs and clenched the anklet, ripping it off and away from Gabble. Suddenly Gabble hugged Helix so tight that Helix almost went blue in the face.

"Th . . . th . . . thank goodness! You've released me from the power of th . . . that horrible woman!" The anklet had been put on by Vivienne: Gabble had been in the wrong place at the wrong time, caught by Vivienne's henchmen when Helix had escaped.

The rising suns showed the time: about six o'clock. The suns were getting closer and closer to aligning. Out of the blue, Gibble appeared. Helix's whistle had woken everyone up.

"Ants, ants, squishy anty ants!" he sang as he stomped on many purple ants. "Helix! M . . . me scared! Gibble thought he'd lost you!" He went back to squashing the innocent creatures, oblivious to what he was meant to be doing and to the fact that Gabble was watching him warily from behind a bush. Helix bent down and picked him up, following behind Gibble who was making his way happily back to the others.

Daniel, bleary-eyed from suddenly being woken up, felt that someone was watching him.

"Is anyone there?" he called.

"Only me!" answered Amelia, feeling on edge as she started calling for Gibble who had gone into the hedges some time ago.

"Gibble! Gibble! Come out here this instant, or . . . or . . . else!" Amelia's threat must have worked, but on somebody else. It was the shrunken Grozotas! They started to emerge from the hedges, coming closer and closer, their red eyes glowing. The children huddled together. At that moment, Helix and Gabble appeared.

"Helix, what's happening?" cried Daniel.

"Gibble s . . . save you!" Gibble started to talk in their forbidden language to the Grozotas. This language was from before Vivienne's time and she had prohibited its use by anyone in her kingdom because it had special words which could cast spells, turning evil magic good. The children looked on in amazement as Gibble was chattering incomprehensibly, then the next minute, the Grozotas were back to their normal size and their eyes, which were once a ruby red, now turned a brilliant emerald green.

Before the children had time to run in fear, one of the Grozotas spoke.

"There's nothing to be afraid of—this Amarku here has broken Vivienne's spell on us. We hate her—let's defeat her together! Climb on our backs and we'll take you wherever you want to go."

Believing Gibble had changed the Grozotas to help ruin Vivienne and restore families who had been torn apart by her, Amelia went over to the green-eyed monsters. Helix and Daniel could see Amelia summoning all her strength and courage to talk to them.

"I think we should head back to the river," she said.

Gibble turned and stopped talking instantly when he saw Gabble on Helix's shoulders.

"Ga . . . Gab . . . Gabble! ENEMY!" Gibble cried as he buried his head into Amelia's leg. Helix took Gabble from his shoulders and held him in a cuddle.

"Don't worry, I broke his anklet, he's safe now." Gibble looked up quickly but still clung to Amelia's leg.

"I sorry Gibble, I . . . I didn't want to be . . . evil" Gabble stuttered.

"All aboard!" called the Grozotas. So, starting to trust them, the children and Amarkus climbed on their backs and then they were off.

*　　*　　*

"Ouch! Ouch! Ouch!" Amelia thought to herself as she was jolted up and down on the Grozota's back. Suddenly something in the trees caught the children's eye—apples! They all agreed a short snack break would be necessary.

Clambering down off the Grozotas' backs, they made for a shady spot under a sturdy apple tree, but the Grozotas were off—they had spotted the river and they were gulping the dark liquid.

"I don't think we should drink that vile river water!" Helix said.

"No, I agree!" said Daniel, "pass a bottle from the back-pack, Amelia." The children and Amarkus drank, then suddenly Amelia shuddered as an apple landed in her palm. Just as she was about to bite it, she heard a savage growl.

"Gibble was that you?" she muttered.

"G . . . Gibble did nothing!" Amelia eyed Gabble.

95

"W . . . Wasn't me!" Gabble chittered. Amelia stared at the apple and realised it had grown large fangs! She screamed and Daniel shot up as if he had just sat on a thorn. Amelia broke off in a run and everyone else followed, the apple chasing after them. Eventually more apples joined the pursuit.

Helix grabbed Gibble and Gabble by the scruff of the neck and pulled them behind a log. Amelia and Daniel followed suit. The apples bounded off without a second glance.

Relaxing again, Amelia saw something shining in the grass. She ran over to it and picked it up. It was a locket and it had mud encrusted on it. It appeared to be locked.

"L . . . Looks like . . ."

"Vivienne's," finished Daniel in astonishment, "but what is it doing here?"

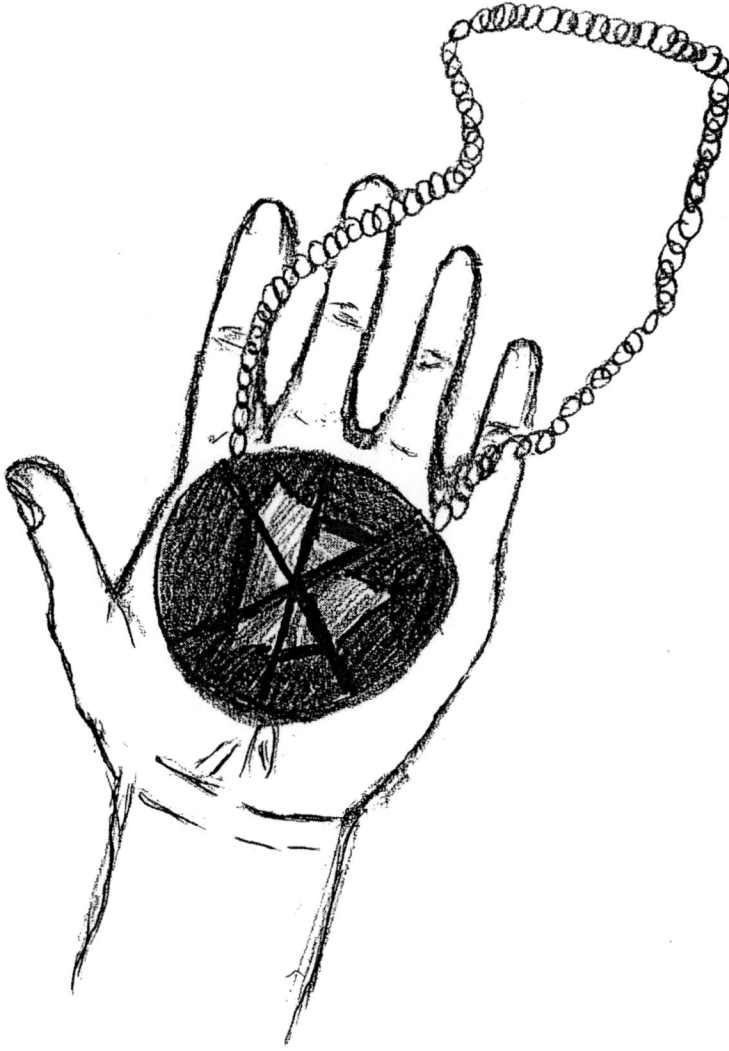

Chapter 7: The Final Hours.

Daniel started searching his pockets only to find them all empty.

"How did it get out?" He looked at the once shining necklace, now layered with mud. Amelia dusted the dirt off and noticed something.

"I'm sure this was pink when you stole it. How did it get out of your pocket?" They all thought for a moment.

"Well it must have fallen out!" Amelia wasn't as optimistic.

"And flown five metres in front of us?" She took off the last few bits of mud and held it up to the suns' light. "Well I hardly believe it'll just fly back to Vivienne!" The locket started to sway a little, "On the other hand I couldn't be so sure, there's too much going on in this world for me to just think it's not down to some spell or another."

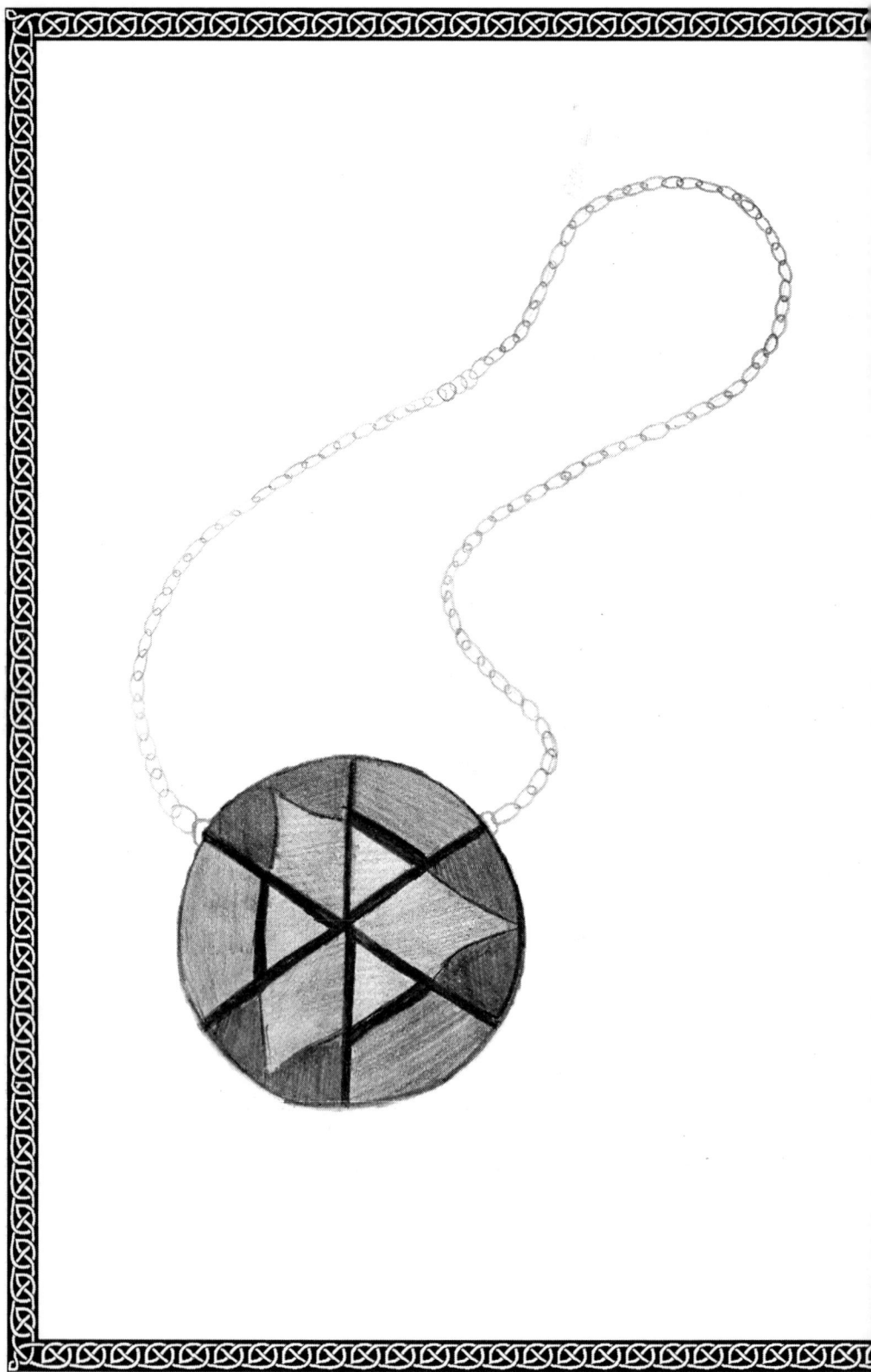

At that point, before Daniel could speak, the necklace yanked itself off into the distance, pulling Amelia to the floor as she had to let go of the chain.

"Grab it!" Daniel called as he ran after it, only to trip over a root a second later. Both on the ground, they saw it zooming away, stopping right at the water before turning a dark murky green and dropping onto the bank. It appeared to take on the camouflage skills of a chameleon.

Scrambling to her feet, Amelia was shouting.

"Get it before it goes again!" Just as it started to shake with movement, Gibble jumped on to it.

"G . . . Gibble save. Yes?" He struggled to keep it under control. Daniel took it from him and held it by the pendant, placing the chain around his neck.

"I guess you were right then, Sis." Amelia smirked at him triumphantly and looked at the suns glittering off the water.

"I remember this . . ." She shuddered slightly at the memory of a terrible storm and creaky boat. "Well seeing as we have a few seconds to spare let's see if we can make a name out of D, R, I, N and N."

Daniel and Gibble nodded in agreement and they sat down together in a circle.

"NRIND?" Daniel suggested, getting a sarcastic reply of "Yes that's it, Nrind!" He sighed and looked back at the letters. After a minute of increasing need for breakfast he decided to give up. "You can make *dinner* if you add an E," he said, clutching his rumbling stomach.

"Now isn't really the time for food! Look at the suns; they're already starting to cross. If we don't hurry up Vivienne will get out and we'll be trapped, watching our world be destroyed."

Daniel looked down sheepishly after that remark only to jump about eight feet into the air when a hand touched his shoulder. "GAHH! Helix!" Everyone sniggered as Daniel calmed himself down.

"Sorry Daniel, I didn't mean to scare you," he said mockingly as Daniel tried to calm himself.

"That isn't funny! Everything's trying to kill us! You can see why I'm on edge." He scowled at his still laughing companions and crossed his arms stubbornly like a child.

"Calm down, it was only a joke!" Amelia smirked as he huffed in annoyance.

* * *

Vivienne picked up her favourite glass goblet and threw it at the wall in a murderous rage. The omniscience potion splashed everywhere; the vision of Gabble being reunited with Helix and the others burned out. She stormed out of her room, screaming at her guards to fetch the Balaur. Within minutes, a scarlet red dragon, hurling balls of deep blue fire, hovered in front of her balcony. It extended a wing to help her climb on to the velvet saddle on its back.

"To the Stockade," she hissed through gritted teeth.

* * *

Amelia and Helix were mumbling quietly to each other.

"You got to go back across the water," Gabble said, creeping up behind them.

"Over to the island? We almost died last time," said Amelia, "why is it we have to go back again?"

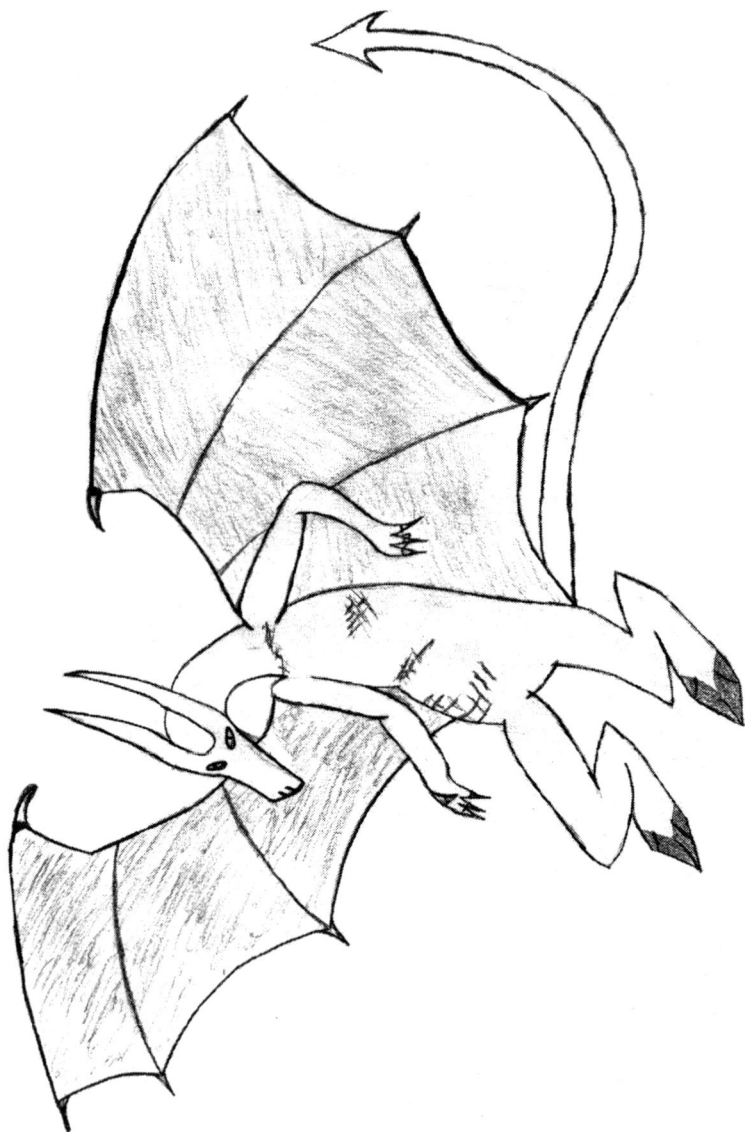

"N . . . no! No! NO! Not again! Staying with Gabble!" yelled Gibble in a tantrum.

"I've found an old boat," interrupted Daniel, "in those thickets. Come on everyone, Gabble's right. I heard Vivienne gloating to the guards at the hourglass about this place, and the locket is trying to get over there."

Amelia reluctantly launched the boat and the two boys grabbed Gibble and Gabble and lifted them in, pushing off quickly before Gibble could get out again. He started to cry.

"Why so mean?" he sobbed.

"We need to stay together," Amelia whispered comfortingly in reassuring tones, even though her voice trembled. Gibble looked up and let out a scream; curling up into a tight ball like a hamster, with one arm pointing upwards, he quivered, "V . . . Vivienne!"

A dark mass obliterated the suns as Vivienne, on her dragon, hurtled down toward them. The Sage, watching closely through the fire, threw a shield over them just in time.

The waters around the boat began to part and arose either side of the small vessel. As they subsided, Gibble began to shriek.

"H . . . hydra! Hydra! Hydra!"

A long scaly neck emerged from the water with a stalk-like tubular body and a ring of tentacles around the mouth. Suddenly the tentacles reached for Gabble, breaking through the shield that had seemed indestructible.

*   *   *

The Sage sighed as he saw that his time to partake in the battle had come. With a wave of his staff he drew smoke from the fire which billowed around him forming a portal to the place to which he had hoped never to return: Vivienne's stockade. The owl saw the Sage enter the portal and with scurrying feet he flew off urgently to the Riddlemaster. The Riddlemaster, engrossed in his towers of books, leapt in fright at the sound of the owl's alarming screech, causing the towers of books to cascade down onto him.

"Master, Master! The Sage requires you immediately. Fulfil the prophecy and be at his side!" Looking round at the chaos that had been his neatly stacked books, which had taken him months to catalogue, the Riddlemaster moaned.

"Oh, my head! Couldn't you have told me quietly and prevented all this mess?"

"The Sage is on his way to the Stockade. Please join him—the battle will soon commence!"

"Call the Scurry then," said the Riddlemaster, slowly standing up, stumbling over the books. The owl let out a mighty hoot and what seemed like a thousand owls descended, landing on the Riddlemaster, grasping him with their claws.

"Don't pinch!" he yelped as they lifted him and carried him off to the Stockade.

The owls flew the Riddlemaster all over the trees, occasionally hitting his feet on them.

"Ow! That hurts!" the Riddlemaster moaned. The owls flew him higher up so it didn't hurt him on his feet as much. They flew all over the place, over the trees, over long grass, over bridges, till eventually they reached the river which blocked the way from the mainland to the island; it was currently calm.

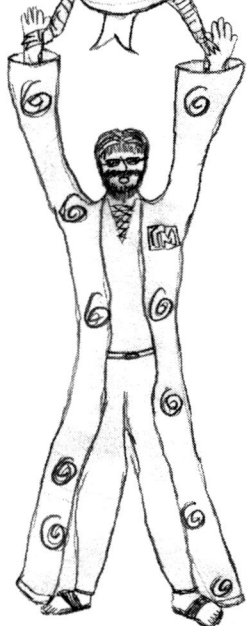

The owls flew him over by the river and when they were hovering near the island's edge, they dropped him from a great height and he landed in the long wavy grass.

"You could have flown lower and then dropped me down! It would have hurt less!" the Riddlemaster shouted to the owls very angrily. The owls just flew further and then landed near some trees. "Now where is the Sage?" the Riddlemaster thought to himself.

Over the river, the Riddlemaster suddenly saw the Hydra in the water, and the twins, Helix, Gibble and Gabble in the old boat trying to get over the river.

*   *   *

Gabble shrieked in terror as the Hydra's slimy tentacles squeezed the life out of him. Helix ran to intercede, hacking with his blade at the tentacle. Gabble broke free, filling his lungs with as much air as he could breathe in at once. Despite his wound, the Hydra rose, enraged with fury: the group looked up in horror as the Hydra descended upon them. He crashed against the side of the boat sending them overboard.

In the distance, the owls heard their cries; they flew back with their wings beating as strongly as ever. Meanwhile, the Hydra moved closer to the group, leaving them with little defence. Helix swam towards it, grasping his sword and attempted to climb its scaly back, just dodging its crashing tentacle. As he climbed, Amelia noticed the tough scales ended near its neck.

"Go for the neck, Helix!" Reaching the neck of the towering Hydra, Helix slashed it through. The Hydra let out a deafening screech. It swayed from side to side knocking Helix off and falling towards Amelia and Gibble. As the Hydra was about to crush them, the owls swooped them up in their talons, then it all went silent: the Hydra had fallen.

Helix whooped triumphantly.

"I did it!" As the owls carried them towards the shore of the Stockade, Amelia looked at the lake, now crashing down onto the Hydra, and gulped.

"How did you do it without any remorse?" Helix shifted slightly in the talons.

"Easy! It went after me first." Amelia bit her lip slightly so she wouldn't say something she'd regret to the person who had just saved her life. They all sighed in relief as they landed and the owls released them.

They looked at the sullen, damp island with the small stone cottage and a forest surrounding it. They gave a slight nod to each other before stepping forward, only to be stopped in their tracks as a cloud of smoke arose from the ground. They huddled in fear, thinking it was Vivienne, only to calm down as the Sage stepped through, clicking his back in several places.

"Transportation always takes it out of me," he groaned, before stretching out a hand to help them up. The children jumped up with a new-found confidence, but only managed a few steps before stopping once more as they were blinded by an outburst of fire. Slowly regaining their eyesight, they looked up and all stopped, terrified of the furious woman in front of them: Vivienne. The Sage furrowed his eyebrows, scowling at his nemesis.

"You never win, Vivienne. Why do you continue to try and escape?" She smirked and directed her gaze to the children.

"So little kids can be put in their place!" she shouted, almost spitting the words out. They backed away a little, except for the Sage who stood his ground firmly.

"Then I think I'll have to give them time to find your name!" Before she could respond, he blasted her with a powerful fireball and she was flung backwards. "Go! All of you! Find the last few letters! I'll hold her off!"

Amelia wanted to protest but before she could even mutter, Daniel had grabbed her hand and dragged her away, with Helix following closely behind. The Sage turned to the coughing witch before him and readied his staff.

"Get up and fight, murderer!" She did and cast an Earth Spell so that vines wrapped around his legs and crawled up his body, slowly suffocating him.

"You're not still upset about that are you? It was many years ago!"

He broke the vines from pure strength and sent her even further back with a Water Spell that also started to sink her into the mud.

"HE WAS MY SON!"

She struggled as the water became heavier, causing the mud to encase her even more quickly. Vivienne struggled and finally released her hand, using a Fire Spell to dehydrate the land around and send it flying in every direction. The Sage shielded himself from the debris and sent an Air Spell at her, forming a powerful mini tornado to smash her against a tree, which promptly snapped at the trunk and began to fall right where the witch had landed.

116

"Timber!" the Sage chuckled to himself as he heard the crashing sound but he knew that was nowhere near enough to kill her. He held up his staff waiting for the oncoming attack but after a minute there was still nothing. Had he actually done it? With nothing but a tree? He edged forward cautiously, watching the fallen tree like a hawk. He was about ten metres away now and he wasn't going any further than that, so using a simple Air Spell, he pushed the tree away and saw its imprint and, oh no, a hole! He dropped the tree and was about to jump into the air when a bolt of lightning was sent jolting up his leg, forcing him to the ground with a yelp of pain.

Vivienne rose like a demon, triumphantly from the ground and held her hand out over his head, smiling wickedly.

"Oh, I am going to enjoy this."

* * *

The oubliette was in the middle of the Stockade; it was dark and filthy and extremely rancid. The prisoner lived in the centre, which was infested with spiders, snakes and flea-covered rats. Filthy water and mysterious brown blobs were strewn across the cold, hard floor. The prisoner fed on the snakes and festering fruit which had been thrown down by the thugs Vivienne called guards. He had to fight the snakes so he could eat them and kill the rats so they didn't feast on his flesh. He had gone slightly mad from near starvation, and he had diseases from drinking the filthy water.

The prisoner was a tall, handsome, young man, with short brown hair, which needed a good wash, and big blue eyes, which looked tired. His face was dirty. He wore a red tartan shirt and blue jeans, both filthy and starting to fray at the edges. His shoes were scuffed and covered in dirt.

* * *

Vivienne's hand started to glow, a bright golden glow, as she combined all five elements into one spell.

"You can't! That's forbidden amongst all Mages!" shouted the Sage. She cackled, knowing it was certain death for him at point blank range.

"Why should I care? You idiots locked me up!" It was almost ready now; he could see it and his breathing hitched and rapidly sped up, which didn't help his crazily, fast-beating heart. He closed his eyes and tilted his head away slightly in anticipation. She released the powerfully dangerous magic but was pushed sideways in the last second by:

"Gabble!" she screeched as she hit the ground, but the Sage still cried out in pain as the spell, although it missed his head, pierced right through his stomach. Gabble started biting Vivienne and she was too weak from casting the spell to face the children now returning. So shoving the Amarku away, she scrambled off to the nearest clump of trees.

Gabble ran to the Sage's side with the others joining and kneeling over him.

"We have to get him some help!" Amelia said in complete panic to the others.

"No, you need to defeat Vivienne! The suns have almost aligned; she must not escape!" His voice was hoarse and he groaned in pain.

"We're not leaving you like this!" Helix exclaimed, adamant in not going, and both Amelia and Daniel agreed. Gibble, although shaking, started tearing different leaves up and crushing them into what looked like dust before placing them on the wound.

"A . . . Amarku—we good h . . . healers." The others were confused until Gabble started helping, much to the Sage's relief.

"We save him! You defeat Vivienne!"

Although reluctant, the three children stood up and started in the direction Vivienne had gone. All they could do was trust Gibble and Gabble to keep the Sage safe.

"He'll be fine, I'm sure!" Daniel tried to reassure Amelia, but she was sick with worry.

Chapter 8: Is It the End?

Vivienne knew the time had come for her to draw in her legions of creatures; she called for Azoth—the leader of the gargoyles.

"Azoth, the time has come for you to mobilise the dark army; the Gargoyles are to form the main defence on the island shores immediately."

"The Gargoyles are prepared and awaiting orders," Azoth replied, "and the Wadu can soon be flocking towards the island shores as well.' Vivienne gave the General an intense stare.

"And what of my Kralj?"

"Oh yes, my queen, your Kralj is heading towards the island as we speak. The Kralj is our best weapon against the enemies; we cannot lose." Azoth spoke with undeniable certainty in his words.

Azoth bowed to Vivienne and flew off to assemble his half of the army. He flew to the tallest tower of the castle and perched on a platform before a garden of gargoyles, frozen in time. He sucked in a deep breath, screeching as loud as he could for several seconds, before panting, "I'm getting too old for this . . ." He waited a moment and watched as the gargoyles slowly started to crumble and their joints became loose. They woke up, cheering for their leader.

After a minute, Azoth flicked his hand, silencing them at once.

"My fellow gargoyles, her ladyship, Vivienne D'Angelo needs our help to win a war against her long-term enemies, the Hunters!" He stopped for effect and to lean in. "Prepare for war!" he shouted, lifting his head high in the air as the crowd erupted again. All that is, except for the smallest of the lot, the runt with whom Vivienne's magic had run out: the baby gargoyle, Achates.

Achates shrank into the crowd, terrified of the idea. He'd been scared of it ever since he was created just ninety eight years previously for that exact purpose. Eventually the gargoyles stopped their noise and started off to the island for the big showdown, marching for assured victory. They had been given their orders by their general only a few moments ago and already the troops were storming through the castle ready to leave. They were to man the shores of the island stockade. But as everyone proudly stomped to the lake, Achates knew he didn't want this side to win; victory for them meant a lot more death around the world and the destruction of Earth.

Azoth, however, needed to get the Wadu as well. He told his second-in-command to keep the gargoyles on track and took off to the darker parts of the forest. Eventually the trees took away any natural sunlight, making giant canopies out of their leaves.

"Kriptotch! Wake up!" For a second nothing happened, then slowly some of the tree bark broke away and an old bat-like creature fell down, gliding at the last moment, landing gently in front of Azoth.

"What is it now, Azoth?!" His tone was agitated and groggy.

"Mistress Vivienne needs our armies for the Hunter War." Kriptotch sighed.

"Well next time, send a messenger and we won't have to talk so much." Although they hadn't really said much at all they had hated each other since their first memory; the only reason they even tolerated each other was because they had undying devotion for Vivienne.

Azoth smirked and turned on his heel.

"Fair enough, just get them to the island," he said, before taking off and disappearing. Kriptotch turned to the ever-darkening trees before sucking in a deep breath and letting it out in a soundless noise, but with a force so strong that trees for miles around were forced back, some almost having their roots torn out from underneath them. Slowly but surely, the bark of a thousand trees broke away as the Wadu army woke up and looked at their leader.

"Vivienne needs us, so wake up and follow me!" he barked, striking fear into all of them. He took off and they quickly followed, knowing the repercussions of being slow.

They arrived at the island after an hour of non-stop flying but even though they were exhausted they still didn't forget the ongoing rivalry between the Wadu and gargoyles. They were still bickering like there was no tomorrow when Vivienne appeared. Kriptotch went to her side as Azoth flew off to find the Kralj.

*   *   *

Opening his eyes the Kralj looked around, dazed from the recent battle. The Kralj had woken. He tried to get up but could not; looking up he saw a large tree upon himself, reminding him of his failure. He cast the tree aside, regenerating his strength. Just then, an evil laugh reached his ear. Turning in surprise, he saw a gargoyle perched up on a hedge with a grin on his face.

"Having a nap are we, Kralj?"

"What are you doing here, Azoth?" the Kralj said angrily.

"Lady Vivienne has asked for me and my army to accompany her; I heard yours has run away. There is a great battle ahead and she has asked for your presence. I don't see why, but I guess you could pull the supply cart."

The Kralj managed to rein in his anger.

"I won't fail this time; tell Vivienne I will be there."

"Oh I will . . . oh and be prepared before talking to her; I don't think she will forget your last fight very easily. Defeated by children! How pathetic!" He flew off in the direction of the island.

The Kralj took time to prepare himself and regain all of his might, and then headed for the island through the dark water. As he arrived, he prepared himself once more and pressed on to Vivienne's camp. All manner of dark creatures had come to her aid. Gargoyles of course, Vivienne's henchmen, the Wadu, the giant bat-like creatures. And the Dragon! Suddenly, his eyes met with Vivienne's as she cast a spell wrapping him in vines. She pulled him in front of her and the spell stopped. Vivienne yelled in anger at the Kralj.

"I told you to kill the children, and not only did they escape but they managed to defeat you as well!" She called him to kneel and moved her mouth as close as she could to his big ears. "I let you live whilst your puny clan fell before my might because you were strong. Fail again and you will be joining them! Now get prepared for the battle!" Vivienne stormed off towards her camp. The Kralj hung his head seemingly in sorrow.

*   *   *

Helix, Daniel and Amelia had several ancient maps and plans spread out in front of them. They had already spent hours focusing on all of Vivienne's army. What would be the best tactic? Who would be able to take down the Kralj? The two Amarkus had done all they could for the Sage and left him sleeping, safely hidden.

Gabble was near the entrance of the cave, away from the centre. He had grown tired of their plans—it would all be useless against her creatures. There were just too many under her control. He shivered, remembering when he was controlled by her.

"If only we could get help."

Helix and the Riddlemaster, who had joined the group, were concentrating on the plans and it was too dangerous for the twins to leave the cave, let alone the island. Suddenly Gabble had a thought and glancing around the cave where Gibble was curled up next to Amelia, whose eyes were drooping, he slipped out, trying not to be seen. He wanted to prove to Helix that he could do this by himself and he could trust him. He knew where to go but it would mean having to get really close to Vivienne's army. Aloud he muttered to himself, "Achates. Where could he be? Achates . . ."

Achates—the youngest of the Gargoyle tribe in battle today—was overwhelmed by the atmosphere surrounding him as the tribe marched into Vivienne's camp. As the young gargoyle was looking around, taking it all in, he caught something out of the corner of his eye . . . A figure, lurking in the shadows. Achates built up his courage and decided to break away from the march to investigate.

Gabble had been waiting for ages. What luck, he thought, as he saw Achates creep over to him. Achates' face relaxed as he saw who was watching him. Gabble knew Achates when he was created and when Gabble and Helix were just about to be trapped, Achates had tried to help. But he was just a baby gargoyle; he hadn't been strong enough to help them then but what about now? He still had a fairly chubby face and his eyes still had a sparkle despite Vivienne and her constant orders. He seemed tired and, though he hadn't grown much in appearance, he had suffered great hardship under Vivienne's rule that had made him grow mentally. Gabble hugged Achates, trying to avoid his oversized wings; he then went on to explain what they had to do and Achates agreed willingly. Anything to stop Vivienne . . .

The thundering of feet pounded across the island as the monsters assembled at their bases. Underground, a young-looking man stared up at a grate confining him to his oubliette. The moons' light shone gently on his tired features.

"The war is here . . ." he said dryly, sliding down the wall feeling the cracks he had made out of anger. "They really have forgotten me, even *her*!" Detest was dripping off his tongue. Suddenly there was a crash, so hard it shook the entire island, and his world lit up with a bright orange glow.

"H . . . hello?" It was a moment before the silence was lifted.

"Hello?" came a child's voice.

*   *   *

When Amelia first saw the mystery man trapped in the oubliette just outside the cave, she was intrigued.

"Who are you?" she asked, "what are you doing here?" Caleb introduced himself and told Amelia that he was a former lover of Vivienne before she turned into a bitter, twisted woman.

"And ever since, she has kept me here as a slave so that I couldn't leave."

Caleb was tired and told Amelia that he never got the chance to get a wash, as Vivienne kept him working all the time and only ever gave him a few scraps of food at the end of the day. She expected him to get up every day and do work for her.

The Riddlemaster peered over the cover. "Caleb, your father missed you!" The man's eyes widened.

"Dad's alive?" He looked directly up and hope filled his eyes. "Help me out, please!" He jumped to his feet and the Riddlemaster waved his hand; an inscription appeared on the wall.

What moves like a snake but doesn't slither at all,
It grows only green on a 60 year old wall?

"What's this?" Caleb asked.

"I cannot help directly; you must answer yourself," he said with a slight smile.

"Well, it's a . . . a . . ." He thought for a moment. "VINE!!" he shouted with glee and just like that the grate was gone and a vine grew from the ground above down into his cell. The Riddlemaster swung down and helped Caleb up the vine.

"Thank you for saving me. Now I need to find Dad." Caleb scrambled to his feet as Amelia explained the whole situation.

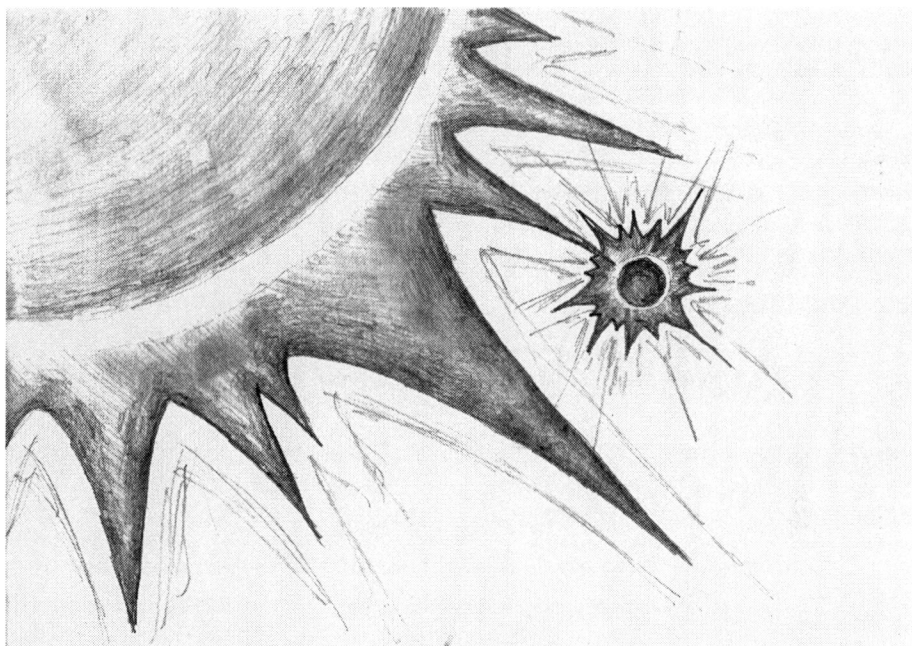

Chapter 9: The Final Beginning

Dawn came all too soon and the time for battle was nigh. The twins looked on anxiously as Helix approached. Their army stared nervously as Vivienne's army began to walk onto the battlefield.

Helix, who was at the front, glanced around their assembled army; he could see Caleb, the Riddlemaster, Amelia and Daniel, Gibble and the owls. His eyes were searching for Gabble. Where was he? He hadn't joined Vivienne had he? Amelia was staring at the growing numbers of Vivienne's army.

"We can't do this," she muttered to Daniel who gripped her hand and said aloud full of determination, "Yes we can! We must!"

It was unpleasantly silent. The only thing that could be heard was the river water crashing against the bones. Helix turned round to face the space between the two armies, looking dismayed. Amelia saw this and whispered mockingly, "Cheer up! You are not afraid of a girl are you? What a wi . . ." but before she could finish her sentence, she noticed something appearing out of the water. She nudged Helix, a smile appearing on her face for the first time that day. Hundreds of Grozotas were stomping out of the water, carrying little Amarkus on their backs. Helix's mouth opened in disbelief. He pointed at a figure flying over the Grozotas.

"Gabble. Look at Gabble! He must have travelled over on that tiny gargoyle and got help."

Gabble was grinning from ear to ear while Achates flew at a slight slant, still not very used to his wings. He hadn't been given the freedom to fly wherever he wanted before. All that was left was for the minutes to pass before they would charge. They waited and waited, Helix beginning to grow eager for the fight. He would finally get back at Vivienne for everything she had done; the pain she had caused.

Both armies were beginning to become uneasy. Vivienne's army began to disperse, allowing a path for Vivienne, the Kralj, Azoth and Kriptotch to move to the front of their army. Vivienne was grinning mischievously; she was going to have a lot of fun. Amelia squeezed Daniel's hand then let go. She didn't want to release his hand as they might not both get through this.

Vivienne's grin widened before she screamed, "Charge!" Her army sprang into action, ready to kill. They seemed so prepared as if they had been training for this for a long time.

The twins' army looked dishevelled compared to them as they sprinted with all their might. The owls swooped over the crowds of angry creatures and the gargoyles were flying smoothly looking for ways to attack. The armies crashed into one another with a deafening sound. The battle had begun!

Azoth landed before the Riddlemaster and smirked.

"Well, the last hundred years hasn't done much for you has it?" Azoth jeered and the other tutted.

"This is a battle not a war, a war implies both sides have a chance of winning, whereas for us, with the twins, means there is no way D'Angelo can win!" he retorted smugly.

Rage boiled inside the gargoyle and he charged at the man. The Riddlemaster skilfully dodged and held his hands out in fighting stance, making the gargoyle laugh.

"Old fool, there's no way you can defeat stone!" He charged again and yet again missed. This was repeated with not a word leaving the man's mouth until he was on the edge of the island; he had a sly smile on his face.

"I can take down the tallest skyscrapers, extinguish roaring infernos and rot away entire lands, yet I can slip right through the smallest cracks, what am I?" The over-confident gargoyle grinned.

"Water obviously!" The Riddlemaster smiled. To one side of him the river lifted and hovered behind him.

"Bingo! Now let's see, what is stone's biggest natural weakness?" Azoth started to back away as he gulped. "Wa . . . . ter . . . ." He turned as the water began to home in on him like a missile.

"Gotcha!" The Riddlemaster laughed before running off to the main battle to help. In the distance, a lot of water encased a group of trees before falling and crushing anything, or anyone, who was under it and then turning to ice.

* * *

Kriptotch flew towards Helix. Helix grabbed a nearby stick so that he could defend himself against the bat-like creature. He swung for the creature but Kriptotch dragged the branch away. He flew back at Helix again and caught his arm, but Helix was quick to react and caught Kriptotch's foot and caused the bat to fall to the ground. They were both injured and needed to rest but Kriptotch was not giving in and got straight back up and flew at Helix in a rage of anger, whilst he was still on the ground recovering from the cut. Suddenly, Gabble leapt in front of Kriptotch as he flew at Helix. Helix shouted, 'No Gabble!' but before he could get to his feet, Kriptotch flew at him and took a giant gash out of Gabble's side. Gabble fell to the ground. Kriptotch turned back to go for Helix for the last time but this time Helix was stronger than ever and grabbed the stick and swung at him with great force. Kriptotch was severely injured and fell to the ground. Kriptotch was out cold!

Helix ran straight over to Gabble.

"Gabble, what did you do that for?" said Helix in despair.

"H . . . e . . . l . . . i . . . x," he said, as he was finding it hard to breath.

"Gabble!! I'm here."

"I . . . did . . . it . . . for . . . you. I . . . wanted . . . to . . . prove . . . how . . . loyal . . . I . . . am."

"But you didn't need to do that."

"But . . . I . . . thought . . . you . . . didn't . . . trust . . . me."

"I do now, more than ever. You just saved my life. Why wouldn't I trust you?" Tears streamed down Helix' face.

"Helix . . . thank . . . you . . . . Tell . . . them . . . all . . . I . . . will . . . miss . . . them and . . . wish . . . Amelia . . . and . . . . Daniel . . . . luck . . ." The last few breaths were very slow and then Gabble was gone.

Helix held Gabble in his arms, very tight. He whispered, "I will always trust you and you will be missed dearly."

Achates watched, a tear sliding down his face. He didn't want to interrupt Helix who had scooped up Gabble's body.

"Goodbye, Gabble," Achates whispered, looking at Gabble's drawn face one last time before disappearing into the distance. Helix placed Gabble down as gently as he could beside a tree. He lightly lifted Gabble's drooping ears and placed them over his eyes.

"Sleep tight," he spoke delicately. He smiled to himself at Gabble's peaceful face, held his paws and remembered him. He sat silently for a minute then stood up, prepared to battle. He would be fighting for Gabble.

Chapter 10: The Suns Align

Gibble stood at the front of the flock of owls, knees quivering. The Balaur, not twenty paces in front, faced him, glaring as if he could see deep into his soul. He wasn't kidding himself, Gibble knew that the Balaur was too strong an opponent, yet this was something that he had to do.

The Balaur spread its scarlet wings and coughed a ball of deep blue fire. In response, the owls leapt off their perches into the air.

* * *

The Sage slowly sat up from the ground. The battle had started, chaos had begun. He looked around taking it all in; Caleb had been watching over him as he recovered. The Sage could hear the squawks of hundreds of owls and the roar of what could only be the Balaur. He began to rise, knowing that he was needed. Caleb immediately rushed to him.

"Father! You must rest! You had a terrible injury."

The Sage surveyed his surroundings to see what was occurring. He saw the Amarkus fighting and a young man watching him. He saw a face that reminded him of someone . . .

"But . . . It can't be!" he said, confused, "I thought he was dead!"

He looked back and forth at the young man time and time again and then said, "It has to be him . . . It's my son!" The Sage began to remember the young man, Caleb, helping him earlier before he had fallen once more into unconsciousness. It was real, not just a lovely dream.

"Caleb! My son!" He reached out his arms and pulled Caleb into them. "Where have you been all this time?"

"I will explain but you must rest. Please!" exclaimed Caleb.

"I am quite aware of my body's recent injuries, however I am needed!" With that the Sage headed towards the sound of the commotion followed quickly by his son.

*   *   *

The smell of scorched feathers lurked in the air as the owls swooped around the dragon. Gibble looked around, panicked, not knowing what to do. He grabbed a rock and pathetically threw it at the Balaur whilst the owls continued to furiously attack the dragon.

That's when it began; the ground beneath the Balaur's feet began to shake. The Sage had come to help.

* * *

Swords clashed, axes shook the ground and the island roared for all the world to hear. Darkness swirled around in the sky and rain fell as violent as the battle, and it fell a crimson red.

Caleb stepped over the hill and saw the mass decimation. A group of Amarkus spotted him and surrounded him.

"Who are you?" they yelled.

"I am Caleb, son of the Sage, I wish to join with you against Vivienne and her forces. I am a friend of the Riddlemaster; he rescued me from the prison and . . . ."

"The prison!! Here, take this!" The small Amarku handed him a breastplate and a short sword. "We trust you Caleb," he said simply.

Caleb drove into the action, slashing at the henchmen with great power. Memories of years of hatred and cruelty from them, making him work, starving him and beating him to near death boiled in his mind. Suddenly a group of Amarkus came flying over his head. A tall man with a golden helmet that had spikes coming out of it and shoulder plates, also with incredibly sharp pointed spikes piercing them, came into view. He held a large mace and he was sweeping Amarkus from side to side, slinging them through the air. It was the jailer, his jailer, the man who had beaten him and laughed as he rotted in the cell: the Captain of the henchmen and the most evil.

Caleb's eyes met his.

"Caleb, finally coming to meet your death!" he said, grinning.

"No! It is you that shall fall, after all the evil you caused and hatred you have spewed from your filthy horrid mind." As Caleb ended his speech he rose up and leapt into the air, crashing down on the Captain with his sword. He was pushed to the ground and as the Captain slammed his mace against the ground, Caleb jumped up and sliced his hand. The Captain dropped his mace and Caleb jabbed him through the chest. The Captain fell to the ground.

*   *   *

The Sage looked around to assess the battle. The Balaur was lashing his tail, swatting the owls off like irritating flies. He gathered his power as he walked closer to the Balaur; the ground began shaking, trees creaking, owls squawking. He lifted up his staff and struck it onto the ground, sending bolts of lightning at the Balaur. They struck his skin which gave a hiss as his eyes searched for the cause of his pain. He fixed his eyes on the Sage and let out a breath of deep blue fire. The Sage used his staff as a shield, throwing the fire back at the dragon. However, the dragon wasn't affected by the raging fire that was rushing around his head. He breathed in deeply, feeling pleasure at the intense heat. He sent more fire at the Sage who was slowly beginning to weaken.

The dragon was standing over the Sage who was on the ground in the middle of gathering a ball of sizzling lightning. This was his last chance but the ball wasn't ready yet. His power was running out.

Flying over the Balaur, Achates was holding Gibble who was hugging two chunks of ice that Achates had collected. He was determined as he screamed, "Now Achates!" Achates swooped down near the Balaur's eyes and Gibble flung the two small boulders into them. It wouldn't stop the Balaur but it would irritate him and give the Sage more time.

The Balaur turned away from the Sage before growling, "AAhh! Who was that?" The Sage had to avoid the Balaur's swishing tail as he stood up and threw the large lightning ball at the Balaur as the dragon turned back to face him. The silver lightning bolts were surging through his body. His eyes were glassy as he froze up and fell onto the ground. The owls rushed away from the toppling body that would have crushed them.

"He is not dead; he will revive in a few hours. He was in a confused state when I hit him so he will be confused about everything from now on," the Sage muttered to Achates and Gibble as they flew over to him.

"But why?" Achates whispered.

"Yeah. Couldn't you just kill him?" Gibble asked.

The Sage rubbed his knees and muttered, "I could have killed him but I didn't. He will not know anything about Vivienne or all the bad things he has done. We can teach him to be good." Gibble looked puzzled and the Sage muttered, "I didn't want to see something else die. It is not their fault, it is Vivienne's. He was a baby like you," he nodded to Achates, "he just got taught to kill and be angry all the time."

The Sage bid Achates and Gibble farewell then left to search for Caleb as Achates nodded understandingly.

* * *

The Wadu and Gargoyles lined up against the Grozotas and Amarkus. They were waiting for someone to start contact and the Wadu were eyeing their 'allies' to see who would go first. It was no contest that they would win against an army of big lizard things and a bunch of fuzzy creatures.

The seconds-in-command of the Wadu and Gargoyles looked at each other and the Wadu commander bowed his head a little and smiled as he mouthed, "Go ahead!" The Gargoyle commander looked at him suspiciously before realising the other side had used the momentary gap to sneak attack and he found himself smashed into the air and into a pile of his own men. The Wadu however had planned for this and kicked off into the air and as the Gargoyles went forward they dived straight into the middle of the action, picking off their prey one by one.

The Amarkus and Grozotas did their best to work together but if the Wadu and Gargoyles kept their distance they were taken down within seconds. They realised they were being surrounded and were soon all trapped in a circle with the Wadu in the air, hovering and the Gargoyles keeping them caged.

"I think it's the Gargoyles who have won this battle!" the Gargoyles declared. They heard multiple hisses from above.

"What do you mean, Gargoyles?! This is obviously our win!" This continued for a while, both sides saying that the other group wouldn't have been able to win the battle outright without them because they weren't strong enough.

The Amarkus and Grozotas just stood there in an awkward huddle before a few around the edges started slipping away and eventually they were in the cover of the forest. The enemy hadn't even realised they were gone and had started a full-on violent fight with one another.

"We can't just leave them there," piped up an Amarku standing at the edge of the forest.

"Yeah . . . I guess . . . Anyone got any rope?" a Grozota replied, joining him and smirking. The others looked at them in surprise, then delight, and from there on they began to take charge. They didn't have rope but vines from the trees did the job and before long they had tied at least one Gargoyle to a Wadu just to see how they'd react. They were the trapped ones this time and as the Grozotas stood there proudly, each with an Amarku sitting on his back, they all started laughing in triumph, which annoyed the tied ones no end.

"What shall we do with them?" an Amarku asked, "How about . . . the Gargoyles go in the river? Being stone they'll fit right in and the Wadu, well maybe they need a sun-tan." He gave a little smile as the captured started to panic slightly.

"Sounds like a plan," the Amarku said, giving the sign for the others to start.

By the end, they were quite pleased with themselves; it turned out, teamwork does pay off. Gibble, appearing on the scene with Achates, could not help but perform a little dance of delight.

* * *

The Kralj bowed down so Vivienne could dismount; the twins entered the clearing, several Grozotas at their heels.

Vivienne smirked, "So you've finally dared to challenge me then? I must admit you have come further than some of the previous twins who have attempted to end my reign." A smug smile formed on Vivienne's face. "However you shall not ruin my plans and so this is where the Hunters fall," she jeered, motioning to the Kralj who was baring its teeth and running its snake-like tongue across them. The Kralj entered almost like a puppet, an angry puppet at that. The children stayed strong and the Grozotas stepped forward a little, giving them support and protection.

"And they have our King," the Grozota which had taken command sneered to his supposed leader.

"Only because you are TRAITORS!" the Kralj roared and the other Grozotas shrank back, but the leader stayed strong with the twins.

"They are on the right side!"

"We're trying to save thousands of people whilst she wants to destroy them!" Amelia spoke up.

"Kralj dispose of these . . . vermin!"

"No!" Amelia shouted, "Look at you; you have let yourself be enslaved by this evil woman. Look at your fellow Grozotas, happy together, free! You can be too if you help us. She has twisted the minds of many, but you, you are stronger than this!"

"Yeah, we've never done anything wrong!" Daniel added, only making the Kralj and Vivienne laugh.

"No-one, not even children, are perfectly innocent," Vivienne said between her mocking laughs.

A silence filled the air and the Kralj stopped, with a look of sadness upon his face.

"Well, go on then!!" Vivienne shouted, breaking the silence. "You are just a pathetic beast; you serve me and you know that. I am your queen. Don't listen to these children and get rid of them before I put you down!"

Daniel thought for a moment then furrowed his eyebrows.

"Fine then!" He looked at Amelia and held out his hand. "The locket," he whispered. Amelia took out the locket they had taken from Vivienne's keep and gave it to Daniel. "This is the worst thing I've ever done and you deserve a lot more than a necklace being taken from you!" Daniel exclaimed, holding the locket by its chain and it began to spin slightly.

Vivienne's eyes widened.

"Give that to me!" she yelled and Daniel pulled it back.

"Why should I?" he retorted harshly. Vivienne regained her composure and turned to the Kralj.

"Kill them and get that locket, then maybe your punishment won't be as bad." Her voice was dangerous and tipped with ice. She expected a terrifying roar to pierce the dreary silence but nothing happened. She turned to find the children confused and the Kralj giving a questioning look. "You're not seriously thinking of defying me are you?" she hissed as the Kralj lowered his head to her level. Silence fell again and you could just make out a word from the hushed deep voice of the Kralj.

"You are wrong, D'Angelo." He narrowed his eyes.

"No!" she cried.

With swift rage, he knocked Vivienne flying against the tree.

*   *   *

The locket, still held by Daniel, began to spin faster. Amelia's eyes widened; three letter 'A's became clear. As the locket spun faster, Vivienne's eyes narrowed in fury and she tried to snatch it away before the twins could see, but she was too late. She looked up, the suns were aligning, she was running out of time. She had failed again.

It was then that Amelia shouted out Vivienne's real name, a name she hadn't heard since she was a child.

'ADRIANNA!'

And with that the suns aligned.

*   *   *

The twins watched as the suns began to glow with a blinding white light and within that light, Vivienne seemed to have disappeared.

The children stood there, wide-eyed and slowly turned around; they saw the light spread as Vivienne's darkness began to lift.

"We . . . won?" Daniel asked, tentatively.

"Yeah . . . we did!" Amelia jumped with joy.

The Kralj bowed.

"Thank you for setting me free." Amelia smiled widely.

"We couldn't let her win! And if you hadn't helped, we'd have lost!" Daniel was still in shock and started laughing in disbelief.

"We did it!" He held his hands in the air in triumph. "We have to find the others." Amelia beamed.

"You don't have to." A familiar friendly voice came from behind and they turned around to see Helix, the Sage, the Riddlemaster, Gibble, Caleb and Achates. Amelia and Daniel jumped.

"She's gone. We won!"

*　*　*

"Goodbye!" Amelia knelt beside Gibble and hugged him tightly, whispering, "I will miss you" into his floppy ear. Gibble's eyes were like little glass balls glistening with tears as he kissed Amelia on the nose and said, "I will always love you Amelia." They were all gathered together in the tent; the Sage was sitting down beside his son Caleb and looking at him, not believing that he could really be alive.

Helix and Daniel were chatting quietly in the corner.

"We could have been great friends if I could stay," Daniel thought, "but he would never be my best friend; that would always be Amelia."

Daniel stood up and glanced at Amelia. It was time to go. They had done what they had to do and they had to get back into the real world. Amelia nodded, then hugged Gibble one last time. She then hugged the Sage and jokingly said to Caleb, "Now look after him. He is losing his touch, the older he gets." Caleb laughed then shook hands with Daniel.

The Riddlemaster said goodbye to Amelia and Daniel then disappeared into the evening light. Things had to be sorted out and they needed to be done as soon as possible.

Goodbyes were exchanged then Amelia clutched Daniel's hand and followed Helix out of the tent. They travelled over the waters in silence. Helix was slightly moody; he had grown to love Amelia and Daniel. They were almost like family and he thought they were going to be together for ever. The twins were leaving; Gabble had gone. He thought he would be lonely but the twins knew the Riddlemaster would take care of him.

The Riddlemaster was sorting out his books that very second. He had to make room for Helix so he could stay with him. Amelia was shivering and muttered, "How long? Where do we have to go now, anyway?"

"Just a few minutes more. We just have to get back to where it started. There will be a force that will drag you back through. At least, that is what the Sage said would happen," Helix answered.

They had arrived at where it had all begun. Little heads were poking out of the bushes, their eyes wide with worry.

"Where are our parents?" one bold girl asked, sweetly. Amelia knelt down and smiled.

"Your parents will be home soon. Vivienne is gone."

The little Amarku nodded, motioning for all her friends to reveal themselves. Dozens of Amarkus watched as Amelia and Daniel were drawn back into the attic.

Epilogue: Seventeen Years Later

As Amelia closed the cover of her book her youngest daughter Zoe asked, "Did this really all happen to you and Uncle Daniel?" Amelia chuckled.

"Well Zoe, it started when we were ten, didn't it Daniel?" Daniel walked away from the window and answered, "It was an adventure of a life-time which will unfortunately never happen again."

Daniel's oldest son, a four year old named Harry, smiled and asked, "Will it ever happen to us?" Daniel walked over to him.

"No, Harry. It won't happen to you because firstly you don't have a twin and secondly the mirror was repaired by your grandfather and locked safely away. History will not be repeated."

"Oh, OK," Harry mumbled. Amelia's eldest, Shelby, gave Amelia a big hug and then went over to her baby cousin and picked him up.

"Did you manage to go back to say goodbye before the mirror was repaired?"

Amelia sadly replied, "Unfortunately no, but actually I managed to get something out so we can be with them always." She held out her hand in which lay Adrianna's locket. Amelia opened the locket and she could see the mirror world and Gibble waving. The children gasped with delight and leaned forward for a better view, waving and blowing kisses at Gibble.

Much later they left their parents and ran off to play, and in the corner of the attic, the mirror sat, glowing beneath a layer of dust.

And many years later, a crack began to appear . . .

Meanings of Names

- Achates—Friendly
- Adrianna—Dark one
- Amarku—Furry one (Ink Link creation)
- Amelia—Hardworking
- Azoth—Mercury (coming from Arabic; means poisonous)
- Balaur—Dragon
- Caleb—Courageous
- Daniel—Keen-minded
- Grozota—Abomination
- Helix—Desired Change
- Kralj—King
- Kriptotch—Shadow (Ink Link Creation)
- Vivienne—Full of life
- Wadu—Derived from the Japanese 'Waru' which means evil

The Ink Links

Alex *
*

Michaela

olivia

Skye Thornton *

louise

Hannah
x — x

Ellie ★

Sara

Naomi ♡

The Ink Links

Holly .F
Higgs

Katie. V. ✡

Eleanor
x

Marcus

Lucy. Y.

Katherine
-x-

Lightning Source UK Ltd.
Milton Keynes UK
UKOW041120070113

204518UK00003B/553/P